Inside the Palisade

Inside the Palisade

K. C. Maguire

Winchester, UK
Washington, USA

First published by Lodestone Books, 2015
Lodestone Books is an imprint of John Hunt Publishing Ltd., Laurel House, Station Approach,
Alresford, Hants, SO24 9JH, UK
office1@jhpbooks.net
www.johnhuntpublishing.com

For distributor details and how to order please visit the 'Ordering' section on our website.

ISBN: 978 1 78279 715 9
Library of Congress Control Number: 2014959602

A CIP catalogue record for this book is available from the British Library.

Design: Stuart Davies

Printed and bound by CPI Group (UK) Ltd, Croydon, CR0 4YY, UK

To M.E. Breen

who was there when I first put pen to paper (and ever since).

Chapter 1

Gamma has stood me up again. I glance at the communicator on my wrist to check the time, tapping on the glass with a chipped fingernail. The other girls are already packing up their lunches, dumping apple cores and handfuls of cherry pits into the composting unit in the corner. This breakroom is a new innovation, a converted storage area that can no longer store anything due to flooding. I suppose the powers-that-be don't mind if the workers get flooded, as long as the dye is saved.

The room empties as the girls wander off to take advantage of the last few minutes of the break. There's only a handful of the hundred or so women from the day shift left hanging around the benches, watching news updates on the wallscreen. The headlines are always the same. The shortages continue, but it's nothing to worry about. The weather? No rain in sight. We're lucky we have a good irrigation system for the farmlands. I look through the grimy pane of glass that serves as the one point of natural light. The rest of the illumination is provided by overhead bulbs that aren't replaced as often as they should be.

Stretching the sleeve of my tunic over my wrist, I wipe a layer of grease from the window and press my eye to it. No sign of my best friend amidst the girls smoking on the patch of dirt outside. I glance with some jealousy over their heads to the farmland in the valley below. I wanted to be a farmworker when I left school, but my mother preferred a more contained environment. Now I'm trapped in this clunky old factory, reverberating with the sounds of machinery while the farmwomen get to soak up the sun. Clad in loose fitted smocks and broad-brimmed wicker hats, they pick apples in the orchards. If I squint into the far distance, I can make out the dark line of the palisade, marking the boundaries of our existence. I wonder if there's anything green left out there. Perhaps we are all alone, an oasis in the middle of a wasteland. A barren desert said to be filled with hordes of *demen*. If they haven't all died out. Victims of their own destructive urges.

The buzzer startles me and I bang my forehead against the glass. Someone sniggers, but I ignore her. I haven't worked here long but have already gained a reputation for being less than graceful. Like at school. Sliding the untouched nutri-bar into my pocket, I head for the door. Its hinges are askew and one panel bangs against the other as I walk through. The factory floor opens out before me. It's still a little overwhelming: ancient machines chugging and churning, floor pulsing with their rhythm, tracking the time like a giant clock.

"Omega!" It's my supervisor, Tau. Her voice is unpleasant at the best of times and even more grating when amplified from thirty feet away over the din of the machinery. She looks like a pug, small and wrinkled. "If you're not doing anything useful, go and get some dye."

A verbal response is pointless against the noise, so I give her a thumbs up and head for the staircase at the far wall. I know what color she needs. Olive. The color of my skin. And the farm workers' uniforms. We're providing for them today.

Sweat beads on my brow as I walk up the stairs, using the twisted guardrail for support. I've never liked heights. The creaking of the metal beneath my feet makes me nervous. With the shortage of engineers, no one has the time to monitor the condition of little things like stairs, but it's as easy to die from a fall as from an engine malfunction. They used to keep the dye on ground level in what is now the breakroom until a rusty pipe burst. Now we keep it in the rafters and send it down on pulleys. Mom says we can expect more of this: stuff breaking down, impossible to repair. She thinks our society is eating itself up. Maybe she's right. Our clothes are patched more often than replaced, and in my last cycle at school, they stopped sweetening our milk with chocolate powder. Patched clothes I can deal with, but I miss chocolate. At least we still have milk as long as the irrigation systems hold up and we can maintain our herd of cattle.

At the top of the walkway, I swipe my communicator over the keypad to open the storage room door. The dimly lit space is divided into rows of clearly labeled shelving each containing barrels of dye in different sizes and colors. The light bulbs pop and spark as I make my way to the inventory screen. A number of bulbs have blown here too, and haven't been replaced. Most of the outside areas are fully converted to solar light, but the inside hasn't fared so well. Not enough engineers to do the conversion.

I punch a request for the dye into the monitor. After a brief hum and a burst of static, the screen displays the location in flickering green type by row and shelf number. Naturally, it's at the farthest end of the room. I grab a mobile platform. It shudders and drags until I remember to kick off the brake. That's when I hear a throaty moan somewhere ahead of me.

Great. I'm not alone.

"May-*gah*, where's that dye?" Tau's voice crackles through my communicator. The moaning stops, replaced by loud whispers and the unmistakable rustle of clothing being adjusted.

I press the button to respond. "On its way."

Two figures emerge from the shadows. Their faces are flushed as they straighten their tunics. One of the girls is thin and blonde. The other is Gamma. Of course. I should have known my best friend would be here when she stood me up for lunch. The storeroom is kind of like her private office, the place she likes to go to avoid actual work.

The blonde glares at me. *Chi Enne*. One of the girls who makes fun of my gawkiness and frequent daydreaming. She flicks a lock of her golden hair over her shoulder and puts on an affected cough, as if my presence offends her. Involuntarily, I run a hand down my own scraggly braid, pulling away at the feel of the split ends.

Gamma's out of breath, cheeks crimson. She adjusts her belt, accentuating her generous curves. Her brown eyes sparkle, and tendrils of her dark hair escape from her braid. Looking at her perfect features, punctuated by a smattering of freckles across her nose, I can't help wondering how she ended up in the factory. She must be destined for something greater. She claims not to have found her Calling, but when we were younger she had her heart set on a glamorous research job. Her mother could arrange it for her, given their clout. She definitely has the brains for it, even though she hides them behind a flirty front. Sometimes I wonder how much of her antics are just for show. We've been best friends forever, but there are parts of her she doesn't share with me.

"I was getting some dye," I say, as if I owe them an explanation.

Chi turns to grasp Gamma's elbow. "C'mon, let's get out of here." She starts to steer my best friend to the door, but Gamma pulls away.

"Give us a few minutes?" Gamma sounds playful, but Chi frowns at her. "I'll be right behind you. I promise." Gamma runs a thumb along Chi's cheekbone.

Chi glares at me before leaving. As the door closes behind her, the lights buzz.

"I'm *so* sorry." Gamma rushes over to me, eyes wide and innocent. "I know I was supposed to meet you for lunch, but then Chi, well, we lost track of time."

"Not really my business, is it?"

"Don't be like that. We just hooked up on smoke break."

"Gamma! Your mother would kill you for smoking."

"Oh, relax." She nudges my shoulder with her own. "I only took one drag. I wanted to see what it was like, you know, before we run out of cigs altogether."

I glance at the shelf numbers, trying to focus on what I'm supposed to be doing. Reaching for the platform, I drag it behind me down the aisle. It jerks to a stop, causing me to lose my grip as Gamma bounces on it to weigh it down. I turn to face her, hands planted on my hips. She's only inches away. Standing on the platform, she's almost as tall as me.

"What are you doing?" I try to scowl but her grin is infectious. Her honeysuckle scent infuses the air around us. Despite the shortages of everything else, most of the girls have figured out how to make their own fragrances from the flowers available inside the palisade.

"Nothing." She looks down at my fingers wrapped around the platform's handle before looping her three middle fingers around mine and tugging, the way she did when we were kids. "Sorry about lunch," she says again, before leaning forward and pecking me on the cheek. I bat her away, but she dodges me. I've never known how seriously to take her flirtations. She only ever seems to be joking around with me, but I don't want to lead her on. I've never felt that way about her, about anyone. Maybe there's something wrong with me.

I sway on my feet and grip the handle of the platform.

"Omega, what's wrong?" Gamma says.

I swallow and shake my head to clear it, blinking in an attempt to get the world back into focus. A pool of sweat dampens my undershirt between my shoulder blades. "I'm okay." My voice comes out shaky. "Just a dizzy spell."

"No wonder. I bet you didn't even eat today. Here, let me help you." She drops from the platform and moves me aside to take the handle herself in one hand while rubbing my arm with the other. Her touch is soothing. The honeysuckle fragrance intensifies.

"Where are we headed?" she asks. I point to a row up ahead and start to move forward, slowly at first to make sure the dizziness has passed.

Gamma continues to drag the platform as we move. "Did you eat anything for lunch?" she asks. "I bet you're not feeding yourself while your mom's away. Any update on when she's coming back?"

"I'm not sure." Mom didn't tell me how long she thought she'd be gone. There's no way of knowing really with these retreats. Motherhood was her original Calling but that job is done now. So she signed up to attend the retraining retreat at the far opposite end of the compound from the housing quarters. It's supposed to be based on the vision quests of long dead inhabitants of our world, to help women find a new direction if their initial Calling is fulfilled. No one is allowed to enter unless they have been admitted to the retreat, and the participants are never permitted to speak about the details of what they experience there. There's no fixed timing for a woman's stay there. It all depends on her individual quest.

"What do you think she'll end up doing?" Gamma says. "Wouldn't it be funny if she ended up in the factory with us?"

"That would be too weird," I say. I love my mom, but there's only so much togetherness I can take, particularly given how over-protective she can be when it comes to me.

"Seriously, are you doing okay without her?" Gamma asks, narrowing her eyes. "You're definitely not eating. I swear you've lost weight since yesterday, and you were already such a beanpole. I knew you wouldn't eat if your mom wasn't feeding you." She shakes her head. "You're coming over for dinner tonight. No arguments."

"May-gah!" Tau's voice blares through the communicator on my wrist. "Where's that dye?"

Gamma makes a face as I lift the device to my lips. "On my way."

"Is Gamma up there with you? She's supposed to be on the line."

Gamma sticks out her tongue as I reply, "Yes, ma'am."

"Send her down here at once."

Gamma makes an exaggerated salute and hurries away. As the door closes behind her, she calls to me, "Remember. Dinner tonight."

Once I have the dye barrel in place, I yank the lever to engage the pulley system and head for the door. The cables strain against the weight as the load descends. By the time I return to the factory floor, a crowd has gathered around one of the machines. No one's working. Tau paces back and forth, arguing with someone on her communicator. Probably her own boss. She beckons to me when she sees me. I drag myself forward, reluctant to hear what she has in mind. Her voice echoes in the absence of the machine noise. "We have a problem. There's a blockage in the valve."

Wonderful. They're going to make me do something stupid and dangerous to fix it.

"We need you to get in there and work it loose," she says.

"Why me?"

"You've got the spindliest arms."

At least I'll only be risking my arm. A week ago, she made me climb into one of the engines. The power was off and the safety was on, but I was terrified all the same. I follow Tau to the machine, and she indicates the source of the problem: a small valve that has been partly jimmied open with a crowbar.

"Take a look," she says.

I press my eye to the opening. There's definitely something there that shouldn't be. It looks like a bolt might have worked itself loose and become jammed. I roll up my sleeve and thrust my arm inside. It's a tight fit, but I manage to slide my fingers along the shaft of the offending item. It gives a little. If I can get my hand around it, I can probably tug it aside. A wave of conversation swells behind me. Tau is close by, but she's talking into her communicator again.

Running my fingers down the bolt, I attempt to pry it loose. Finally I get a decent grip, and tug. It doesn't budge. I try to wiggle it from side to side. No progress at first but eventually something gives as I twist and pull at the same time. Taking me by surprise, the bolt jerks free. The momentum pulls me backward. I'm sure I'm going to crash to the floor, but my body halts mid-motion, my arm jammed in the valve, pinned there by the bolt I've been trying to move. Someone gasps. A pair of hands clamps over my arm and starts to yank. Tau is trying to free me, and not very gently.

"Stop!" I scream. I've never raised my voice to her before, but she's hurting me.

"I can't." Her whisper chills me. I hear the beep, followed by a distant humming. She's already given the order to restart the machine. They're going to turn it on with my arm inside.

Chapter 2

The thrumming becomes louder as the machine churns to life. It was stupid for Tau to have given the order to restart it, but it takes a few minutes to get it going. She must have thought we had enough time. I feel, rather than hear, vibrations rumbling through the mechanism. Tau is breathing in hard desperate gasps beside me. Several girls have joined her tugging at my arm. Others yell in the background.

"Call the manager!" My voice is lost in the commotion. All I can see is the gray metal bulk of the machine, pinning me in place as frantic hands pull at me from behind. It feels like forever before I hear a soothing voice at my ear.

"Don't worry. We called her. She's shutting it down."

Gamma.

A moment later, the vibrations subside and the pressure on my arm eases as the machine stutters to a stop. The smell of steam and sweat surrounds me as the girls work to pry the valve open. I drop my head back to see the cracked plaster ceiling high above me, as the workers begin to hoist me backwards.

"Easy, easy. Don't break it." Tau's voice is frantic.

"Can't you see she's hurt?" Gamma's angry now. "Don't worry," she says to me. "It's going to be alright." My arm slides out of the machinery and I tumble into a pair of waiting arms. Gamma lowers me to the floor as the other workers crowd around us.

"Let me see." She maneuvers my arm into her lap and I wince in pain. I raise my head to look. There's a lot of blood, and I have to turn away. Girls are murmuring nearby.

"You're such a wuss," Gamma says, but her words are strained. She calls out to someone in the distance. "Where's the Med-Kit?"

"Coming," Tau's voice belts out from somewhere near the

back of the factory.

"Someone call the Clinic." Gamma says. "Tell them we have an injury. We'll need a transport."

"No," I manage to stammer. I don't want to be carted off by emergency services and have everyone stare at me and tease me about my clumsiness. And have my mother find out how much attention I managed to bring down on myself while she's away.

"Omega, you're hurt. We need to get you to the Clinic." The injury must be bad. Gamma sounds worried and the other girls are crushing in to get a closer look. I hear a few gasps and then a loud grunt as Tau pushes Gamma aside and takes her place beside me. Her brow is drawn and she's brandishing a Med-Kit. She kneels down and grasps my arm none too gently. I stifle a cry.

"Damn. This looks bad," she says. I have a feeling she's more worried about her job than about me. The supervisors lose points when girls are injured on their watch. "Move back, ladies. Give me room to work."

The press of the crowd diminishes as the girls split off into groups around the factory giving me a chance to view Gamma standing directly behind Tau watching her work on me. My arm starts to sting as Tau disinfects the wound. I'm not watching what she's doing, but the smell of antiseptic burns my nose. Gamma walks around behind me and her arm snakes over my shoulders as she cradles me against her. Her honeysuckle fragrance combats the medicinal smell. I can't help burying my nose into her tunic for comfort. A wave of dizziness engulfs me, and I focus on breathing until it passes. Moments later, Gamma braces my cheek with her hand and tilts my head so I'm facing her. A girl I don't know passes her a white capsule and a glass of water.

"A painkiller. To take the edge off," she says.

I reach out for the pill and slip it in my mouth. Gamma presses the glass to my lips so I can chase it down with a swig of cool, clear water. After I swallow, she removes the glass and smoothes my hair back. She's calmer than she was. "It's not as bad as it looks, Omega. The cut is long. That's why there's so much blood. But it's not very deep."

It doesn't hurt as much anymore. Maybe Tau is being more careful, or maybe the painkiller is kicking in. Within a few minutes, I can feel her wrapping the injury. She's tying the bandage so tight my arm tingles. I inhale sharply and turn to watch her. Her knuckles are as white as the bandage. Gamma continues smoothing my hair, like my mother did when I was little. She turns to someone behind her and asks, "Is the transport on the way?"

"No." This time I manage to make my voice stronger and I force myself to sit up as Tau ties off the bandage. I can see that the groups of girls have now dispersed further around the factory. Some seem to be missing, probably outside taking a smoke break while they have the unexpected opportunity.

"It's not so bad, Omega, but we do have to get you to the Clinic," Gamma says.

"I'll walk." Maybe I can slip back home without anyone noticing.

"I'll go with you." Gamma helps me to my feet. I'm a little shaky, so I lean into her as she wraps an arm around my waist. Tau is kneeling beside us, repacking the Med-Kit.

Tau rises to her feet and rounds on the few girls who are still hanging around the action. "Get back to work. All of you." She turns to us and addresses Gamma who is urging me toward the door. "Where do you think you're going?"

"Taking her to the Clinic, ma'am." Gamma stresses the last word, her grip tightening around my waist.

Tau strides toward us, Med-Kit in hand. "Are you deaf? I said get back to work."

"Ma'am, she won't go if I don't take her." Gamma stands her ground, locking eyes with Tau.

"She'll go." Tau drops the Med-Kit with a clang. "She'll go because I'm going to call ahead and tell them to expect her." She raises her communicator and starts pushing buttons.

"Ma'am, she's hurt." Gamma releases me and plants her hands on her hips. "She won't be able to get there without help."

"She looks steady enough to me." Tau indicates me standing without Gamma's assistance. "You're alright to walk to the Clinic yourself, aren't you, girl?" It isn't really a question.

"So you get back to work." Tau points a stubby finger at Gamma before nodding at the Med-Kit by her feet. "And put that away while you're at it."

Gamma frowns, apparently not planning to push her luck. She snatches up the Med-Kit almost ramming it into Tau's shin in the process. Tau jumps back but it only takes a moment for her to regain her composure. She turns her attention to me. "Get on your way, girl. I'm putting the call in now." As she raises the communicator to her lips, I meet Gamma's dark eyes over her shoulders. Then I turn and head for the exit, the factory's oversized steel doors looming in front of me.

* * *

A wrought iron gate marks the entryway to the Clinic. The three-story building is surrounded by a fence that stretches out around a lush garden. Its centerpiece is a reflection pool set into the ground in a perfect circle. The gate is never closed. It's intended as a signal that those in need are always welcome. The area is tranquil between shifts. The sinking sun's rays dance across the water's surface. At the far end of the pool, there's a woodland comprised of firs and oaks, arranged to provide shade and relaxation for those lucky enough to come out and enjoy it. If only I had time to soak it all in.

A pair of squirrels darts around me, racing each other for the base of an oak tree. One follows the other up its trunk, chittering excitedly until they disappear amidst the leaves. My contact lenses scratch my eyes. I shouldn't take them out in public. If anyone knew, it would lead to questions that I can't answer. My mother says it's only a genetic abnormality, but those aren't supposed to exist inside the palisade. It's better no one knows about my eyes.

With a furtive glance to check that I'm truly alone, I slip beneath the oak tree the squirrels climbed. Its foliage shields me from view of the building down the path. I lean into its rough bark, unable to resist running my palms along its ridges and valleys, immersing myself in its sweet summery scent. If I were a squirrel, I guess this is the tree I'd pick for my home too. After a moment, I crawl to the edge of the reflection pool and lean over the water. My face gazes back at me, a little paler than usual, my mop of chestnut hair escaping from its braids.

The lenses are still in place, their fake blue beaming up at me. I pinch out the plastic discs and clip them into the case I always keep in my pocket. Placing it on a rock beside me, I cup my hands under the water and splash my face, blinking my eyes to lubricate them. The water is cool and refreshing, reminding me of Gamma holding the glass to my lips. I press my fingertips to my mouth. She's my very best friend. She has no problem finding girlfriends. Why don't I feel that way about her? About anyone here? Life would be so easy if I did. My future could be all mapped out.

I could commit to a life partner, have a family and hopefully retrain for a better Calling. Of course, the one Calling I'd like doesn't exist anymore. Adventurer, explorer. Like in the old history books we study at school. If we still had explorers we could find out what's really outside the walls. It can't be empty nothingness forever, can it?

My thoughts are interrupted by a movement in the trees, followed by a flurry of falling leaves. A pair of eyes stares at me from a high perch. Someone is hidden there, masked by the leafy canopy, haloed by the sun.

Is it a girl playing around up there? Or maybe an animal,

although it seems pretty bulky. Too big to be a squirrel. Could be a raccoon, but do they actually climb trees?

I take a breath and call out, "Who are you?"

No response.

"What are you doing up there? Are you stuck?"

The figure shakes its head. It understands me. So, not an animal.

"Why don't you come down? I won't hurt you."

The head shake is vigorous, causing the tree to shed more leaves. I move forward until I'm directly beneath her, but she shimmies to a higher branch.

"Don't be afraid. I'm going to call for help." I raise my communicator to make the call.

"No!"

I don't know if I only imagine the hissed word combined with the whoosh of air when the girl leaps from her perch. She drops like a huge black bat, arms outstretched, draped in something thick and dark. She catches me off guard, pushing me backward. My knee twists painfully, and I feel something tear as I go down, but I can't cry out. The fall knocks the wind out of me.

Then she's on me, clawing for the communicator at my wrist as she straddles my hips and pins me. I try to fight back, but my injured arm screams in pain. With a last violent jerk, the girl succeeds in snapping the communicator strap and pulling the device away. I draw in a breath to cry for help, but her hand is over my mouth, her body pressed to mine. She's unbelievably strong. I thrash against her but she presses down harder making it difficult to breathe. My vision blurs. I'm worried I'll pass out. I try to get a look at her face, but I can't see past the hood of the dark cloak. Focusing on breathing through my nose, I try to steady myself. The girl begins to relax her grip.

"I'm sorry," she says in a low husky whisper. "I couldn't let you call them. They can't find me here." Her hand drops to my shoulder, and I sense her exhaustion in the motion. Is she a psych patient? I vaguely remember Gamma mentioning her mother treating a case a while back, but I've never met anyone suffering from mental problems before.

The girl's hand remains over my mouth, her head pressed down on my shoulder. Her breathing is ragged, warm puffs of air billowing hot against my neck. We both hold still for several moments. Finally she straightens to arms' length, keeping my mouth pinned with her hand and my torso pinned with her legs. As she leans back, the hood flops away, and I see her face for the first time: piercing dark eyes set against large angular features. But that's not what makes me gasp. It's the scruff of fur covering the lower half of the face. I redouble my efforts to fight when I realize the horrible truth. This isn't a girl.

It's a *deman*.

Chapter 3

My fight doesn't last long. I'm hampered by the pain in my knee and injured arm. The *deman* is so strong. He leans in and clamps his free arm against my collarbone. His furry cheek scratches my throat. I can smell the scent of oak on his skin as well as a hint of something else. Lavender? How could he have gotten inside the wall? The palisade can't be breached. Our ancestors sealed it tight generations ago.

He inhales deeply. Is he *sniffing* me? I buck against him. Bad move. A shock of pain screams through my knee, and I cry out against his clammy palm. I'm surprised when the pressure is released from my chest. He's lifting his weight off me but keeping one hand locked over my mouth. He slides the other to my waist.

No! I can't let him touch me there. I know what these *demen* do. I've read the history books. I brace my palms against the ground and grasp at the rocks and stones. Anything I could use as a weapon. There's nothing big enough. He clamps his hand around my upper thigh, causing me to grimace.

"Stop that." His command is hoarse, his grip unyielding. "If I take my hand away from your mouth, can you please keep quiet?"

My eyes widen. He talks like me.

"Look." He releases my thigh and brings his face close to mine. His eyes are dark and unreadable. "Your leg is hurt, but I can't look at it if I have to keep you quiet. We can't stay here like this. Please."

A monster is begging me to cooperate?

"I'm sorry you're hurt, okay? I want to help," he says in that hoarse desperate tone. Abruptly, he slides his free hand beneath my shoulders. I try to resist, but he braces me and pulls me to a seated position. I try to bite the hand over my mouth, but he pulls me against him. This fight is pointless. I can't win. With little cooperation from me, he manages to maneuver me into a seated position on the ground. He has one arm looped across my chest, covering my mouth from behind. With the other, he points at my leg. That's when I see the fabric at the knee of my trousers is ripped. A large swelling rises underneath. Beads of blood pucker around the edges.

"You're injured." The *deman's* voice is surprisingly kind as he manipulates the fabric just above the injury with one hand while holding me in place with the other. I twist my head to face him. When my eyes meet his, I'm surprised to see what looks like a mixture of hesitation and fear. He's younger than I thought, his skin pale with purple hollows beneath his eyes. His hair is shaggy and unkempt, hanging just above his shoulders, the bangs drooping into his dark eyes. "Will you let me help you?"

A bat screeches overhead. We can't sit here like this all night. If he thinks I'm cooperating, he might lower his guard, and I'll be able to escape. I avert my eyes and nod.

He loosens his grip, but hesitates. "You won't scream?" His breath puffs against my skin. Warm and moist. I shudder.

I shake my head. No, I won't scream. If I did, there's no telling what he'd do. What if he's not alone? A chill snakes up my spine as I glance over my shoulder, seeing nothing but the quiet woodland surrounding us. A lizard peers out from under a rock by the water, flicking its blue tongue a few times before disappearing again.

"I'm going to let you go now," the *deman* says, without loosening his hold. "Stay calm, okay?" Ever so slowly, he releases me. I slump forward, forcing myself to resist the urge to bolt. I hold my face between my hands and try to focus, pushing down the bile that rises in my throat. I close my eyes for a moment. When I open them, he's skirted around in front of me, kneeling beside my outstretched legs. Even on his knees, he seems enormous, probably because he's so broad across the chest. He's wearing dark clothes, but they look like the regular outfits we wear in our quarters. Simple cotton trousers and a fitted shirt. Nothing like the animal skins I would have expected from an outsider, a savage. His arms and legs are muscular. He's wearing a short-sleeved shirt so I can see that his arms are a little hairy, but no more than some of the women I've seen in the field.

He *is* younger than I thought. The skin around his eyes is smooth and unlined. He's probably about my age. That would make him a *boy*, wouldn't it? I think back to the terminology from our history classes. The dark circles are pronounced under his eyes. Maybe he's ill. Is that why he's outside the Clinic? Does he need medicine?

He loosens his cloak and drops it to his knees, producing a penknife from the side of his leather boot. I flip over, but my knee buckles, and I fall to the ground. Before I can try anything else, he grabs my good ankle with his free hand and drops the knife. Then he leans over and clutches my shoulder. His face is so close I can smell his sweat again. The hint of lavender mixed with the scent of oak. His eyes search mine, wild and panicked. "Stop."

"What are you doing?" I gesture to the knife with a tilt of my head.

The *deman* kicks the knife away with the tip of his boot, sending a cloud of dirt into the air. "I was only going to make a brace for your knee." He nods at the blade and lifts his cloak from the ground to demonstrate what he was planning. "I was going to cut a strip of this as a bandage for you."

I stare down at the pile of fabric in his arms. His cloak and boots are as well made as the rest of his clothes. They look like something manufactured inside the palisade by our stitchers and weavers, but that's impossible. He looks me over and then makes a grunting noise low in his throat.

"What?" My tone is sharper than I intend, sharper than I can afford under the circumstances.

He leans forward, a muscle twitching in his jaw. "I should have known better than to try and help a stranger. They warned me I wouldn't be safe here. I should have listened."

His words ignite my anger full force. "*You* wouldn't be safe here? That's rich. You *demen* are the ones who hurt us. That's why we built the palisade in the first place."

"That's right. *We're* the evil ones, aren't we? The terrifying *demen.* Not you. Not women." He almost spits the last word. "You can't even say it, can you? What we really are. Human like you. Another gender. Not another species." He sinks back on his heels, dropping his head into his hands.

His voice catches when he speaks again. "Just go." He doesn't look at me. This may be a trick, but he sounds so sincere. I gather my feet under me, grimacing at the ache in my leg. The *deman* looks up at me from his hunched position, accentuating his pale cheeks and the hollows under his eyes. He really does look ill. The fact that he doesn't move any closer stokes my courage, and my curiosity. "Why are you here?"

"I'm waiting for someone." He wipes his sleeve over his eyes. Who could he know inside the palisade? As the sun's sinking rays hit his face I notice a slight asymmetry in his features – the right side of his mouth tilts higher than the left. I press the heels of my hands to my temples. The leaves rustle in the breeze. Tiny ripples line the pond's surface. It's not possible for this creature to be here. But he is. I have to know why. And how.

"Who are you waiting for?" I ask.

He turns his head toward the looming brick building at the end of the path. "Someone in there." The trees cast long shadows against its limestone façade.

"I thought you didn't want anyone to know you were here."

"She already knows," he says as he gathers his cloak into his lap. "Maybe we could help each other?"

I look down at him, sitting there. Alone. Running his fingers through the hem of his cloak, glancing occasionally at the building behind him with what looks like yearning in his expression.

"What did you have in mind?" I ask. I know I should run. Get as far away as I can and report him. I know I should. But this creature is from outside, and he's here. I need to know why.

A glimmer flashes through his eyes. He rises to one knee and snatches for his cloak before it tumbles to the ground.

I take another step back. He holds his arms out, palms upward. "I could help you with your knee." He points at my torn trouser leg. "And you could deliver a message for me." He cocks his head toward the Clinic.

I clasp for the communicator on my wrist only to remember that he never gave it back after our scuffle. "To a Med-Tech?"

Then he surprises me by grabbing for the knife and offering it to me hilt first. I take it from him, hefting its unfamiliar weight in my palms. It's only a small pen knife. It probably wouldn't do much damage to anyone, but the fact he's given it to me seems significant. The corner of his asymmetrical mouth twitches as he begins to tear the edge of his cloak to make a bandage. He holds it out and gestures at my knee. The cut is beaded with blood. I must have scraped it along a tree root or a rock when I feel. The joint is swollen and bruising. The *deman* looks up to meet my eyes and gestures again with the bandage. I bite down on my lip. This is the point of no return. Am I really going to let him touch me? I straighten my shoulders and raise the knife in his direction before jutting my chin down to indicate that it's okay to touch me.

He leans forward, keeping his eyes pinned on mine and raising his eyebrows before hitching up the hem of my trouser leg and rolling it up to my knee. His fingers are warm and calloused. I grit my teeth and grip the knife tighter, but he's not paying attention to it. He's completely focused on the injury, working with confident movements as he braces the joint. Firmly, but not too tight. Like a Med-Tech. I'm almost hypnotized by the sight of the monstrous hands engaging in such skillful work.

As soon as he's done, he rolls down my trouser leg, careful not to jostle the injury and rocks back on his heels. I shake my head in disbelief. He did a good job. My trouser leg is still ripped, but the tear is more difficult to see with the dark bandage underneath.

"Where did you learn how to do that?" I ask.

"That's right. A *deman* wouldn't know first aid, would he?" His brow wrinkles as he inches away from me.

"I'm sorry. I didn't mean—" I force myself to stop. Why am I apologizing to a *deman*? "So what is this message you want me to deliver?"

"Tell her…" He stops to think, glancing briefly at the building behind us. The last of the sun's rays illuminate the edges of the clouds, setting them alight with golden haloes. "Tell her I won't leave without her."

He wants to take a Med-Tech outside the palisade?

"Is that some kind of threat?" I ask.

"Of course not. She's my… Never mind about that. I haven't seen her for three days and I'm worried about her."

"Worried about who? Did she come from the outside with you?"

"What? No, she came from her quarters. I'm sorry. I can't say anything more. It's too dangerous."

"What's her name?"

He hesitates and swallows. "Delta. Delta Jaye."

With that, he gathers up his cloak, turns on his heel and heads for the tree line. Then he turns back to me. "Could I have my knife please?"

I extend my open palm, the penknife nestled upon it. He won't hurt me now. He's going to leave. When he takes it from my hand, his fingertips scrape over my skin, leaving a rush of warm tingles on my palm.

"Thanks," he says as he slips it into his belt.

"Wait." I begin to follow him before I can think better of it, but he's too fast. He keeps moving and by the time I get to the trees, he's gone.

"Who are you?" I ask softly into the darkness. "What's your name?"

The only response is the rustling of the leaves and a few splashes in the pool, probably catfish surfacing to look for food.

I need to get moving too, before someone starts looking for me. Tau called ahead and I've wasted too much time. My leg aches but not too badly for me to walk if I take it slow. The brace is actually helping a lot. As I turn for the path to the Clinic, I notice the plastic case on the boulder. I'd forgotten about my contacts. And the *deman* never noticed.

Chapter 4

The harsh fluorescent light in the Clinic's waiting area stings my eyes. My contact lenses are scratchier than ever, but I can't do anything about that. The room is compact with orange plastic chairs crammed along every wall except for the one farthest from the entryway. That one houses the glass window to the receptionist's cubicle. Beside it is a door to the examination rooms. I'm the only patient here.

I had to play a round of twenty questions with the receptionist when I couldn't produce my communicator for identification. In everything that happened outside, I didn't think to ask the *deman* to return it. Most of the buildings inside the palisade were set up originally to scan the signals from the devices every time we went in or out. These days, much of that tech. The engineers' to-do lists are getting so long that it takes forever to fix things like this.

I told the receptionist that I had lost my communicator at the factory during the accident. What's bugging me is what I *didn't* say, and why. I had thought about turning in that *deman,* raising the alarm, but I couldn't do it. There was something about him, something lost and helpless. And there was the mystery of Delta. Who was she and how did he know her? Had she been outside the wall? Did she know what was out there?

I stare at the door leading to the examination rooms. It's clearly been painted over many times. Layers of chipped white paint peek out through the latest rough veneer. The door opens with a creak and a tall thin figure in a white tunic glances around the waiting area until her gaze fixes on me.

"Omega Wye?" She smooths down her gray hair and glances at the datapad propped in the crook of her arm. I raise my hand, not sure why I bother given the lack of other patients.

"My name is Rho Zee," she says. "Follow me, please."

Hissing against the pain in my knee, I stand up. My leg throbs when I put weight on it. The Med-Tech directs me through the doorway and leads me down a maze of gray and white corridors to a sparsely furnished examination room where she motions for me to sit on a metal bench. Turning her attention to her datapad, she summarizes my stats. "Omega Wye. Age: Eight-hundred-and-forty-three weeks. Mother: Sigma Wye." She pauses. "Accident at Main Plant. Gash on right forearm."

"Yes, ma'am." The room smells sterile with a hint of the same lemon-scented cleaning agent we use at the factory.

The Med-Tech tilts her head before approaching. Finally, she rolls up my sleeve to inspect my injured arm. "Your supervisor did this?" She indicates the now-seeping dressing. "What about this?" There's pressure on my knee, and when I can bear to look again, she's rolling up my trouser leg to expose the bandage. I realize immediately what has piqued her interest. Under the harsh lights of the examination room, I notice the fabric for the first time. It's a deep crimson, shot through with fine gold thread. I hadn't been able to make out the details in the dim light outside.

Rho Zee examines her datapad. "The report doesn't say anything about a knee injury."

"It happened when I fell," I say.

"At the factory?"

"Mmm-hmm."

She runs her fingertips across the *deman's* handiwork. "This fabric is unusual." She glances up at me and I try to keep my expression stony. "And it looks familiar. I've seen it on a friend of mine." She leans closer. "You wouldn't happen to have come across a Delta Jaye, would you?" The words sound casual, conversational, but her lower lip quivers.

My pulse quickens, but before I can respond, the Med-Tech's communicator buzzes at her wrist. She presses a button to open the comm-channel.

"Everything alright in there? Do you require assistance?" An unfamiliar voice crackles into the room.

"Everything's fine. Re-dressing a wound," Rho Zee answers.

"Carry on then." The communications channel snaps off, disconnected at the other end.

The Med-Tech locks eyes with me, her face ashen.

"Do you know Del—?" The Med-Tech presses a hand over my mouth to stop my words before holding a finger to her lips. I nod that I understand. She steps back and turns her attention in an exaggerated professional manner to my knee.

When she speaks again her voice sounds a little too loud. "Let's take a look, shall we?" She strains to untie the *deman's* knot before unraveling the bandage and rolling it into a tiny ball. She slips it into her pocket and then she starts to manipulate my joint. A spasm shoots through my leg.

"I'll need to replace this dressing but we also need to see to that arm." Hoisting my sleeve higher, she loosens Tau's bandage. Flakes of dried blood drift to the bench around me. She moves to a nearby drawer to retrieve a syringe and a vial of clear fluid. I shrink back. Her movements become stilted, her voice more forced.

"I'll need to stitch this up." She indicates the gash on my arm. "But first I'll give you something to help you relax." She advances on me with her thumb poised over the hypodermic. I back away, but my shoulder wrenches against the wall. "This won't hurt." Her tone is detached, almost robotic, as she grabs for my arm. I try to pin it into the corner, out of her reach.

"It's just that I hate needles."

"You don't have to watch." She grips my arm and pulls it closer, causing a line of blood to seep from the jagged cut. She dabs something cool and moist across my shoulder. An antiseptic wipe. The sharp point of the needle pierces my skin.

"Try to relax." Her voice sounds like it's coming from far away, even though she's right next to me. I want to protest but my jaw muscles have gone slack. I glance at her, but I can't make out her features anymore. Everything is blurry. Rho's strong arms brace me as she lowers me onto the bench, raising my legs so I'm lying flat. She arranges my arms by my sides. I want to cry out, but I'm too tired.

I don't know if I imagine her whispered words before I drift off. "I'm sorry. Delta is my friend. I have no choice."

Chapter 5

"Hey! New girl! Are you awake?"

I blink. Eveything's fuzzy. I'm lying flat on my back, barely able to make out the gray tiled ceiling overhead with vent work snaking around the edges. I ache all over, my limbs heavy and sore.

"Hey! Are you alright?" The stranger speaks again, her tone high-pitched. "You were screaming. Did you have a nightmare?"

I turn my head toward the voice, but I can't see her. I try to roll on to my side, but I can't move. Something's pinning me down. I try to fight it off.

"Easy, easy." She's closer now. "Don't worry, sweetie. They tucked you in a little too snug, that's all."

A girl's face sharpens into focus. She hovers over me, loosening a thick pile of blankets from my chest. A rush of cold air invades my lungs, causing me to cough. The girl braces my shoulders and assists me to a seated position, slapping me too hard on the back and causing another spasm to rip through my lungs. When I catch my breath, she grins to expose a set of shiny white teeth, one of them chipped in the front. Her mousey blonde hair, untidily gathered at the nape of her neck with a bright red bow, is streaked with something sparkly and silver. "I thought you'd *never* wake up. What's your name?" Her volume is a bit much, but at least she's friendly.

"Omega." My voice croaks from my dry throat.

"I'm Ace." The grin widens.

"Ace?"

"It's Alpha actually. Alpha See. But I don't answer to Alpha, okay? When are you due?"

"Huh?"

"The Big Event. You're not showing, so you must have a while." Her voice is even louder, like an excited child.

I look around. The room houses only two cots, a wall mirror and a small metal closet with sliding doors. This girl, Ace, smells soapy and clean. She's clad in a dark robe, streaked with the same silver as her hair.

"Do you like it?" She fishes into her pocket and pulls out a glitter pen. "I can do you too." She brandishes the pen in my direction, but I cower away, reaching protectively for my braids. That's when I realize my hair has been brushed out, falling in silky waves around my shoulders. It feels like even the split ends have been tidied up.

"Hey, I don't bite!" She moves in closer with the pen, before stopping short. Her mouth drops open. "Wow, that's amazing!"

"What?" I raise my fingers to my cheeks, feeling for bruises, or other signs of trauma.

"Your eyes! They're unreal!"

My lenses.

Instinctively, I reach for the case in my pocket, but it's missing. In fact, my whole uniform is gone. I'm wearing a pale robe over a scratchy flannel gown. My real eyes are exposed to anyone who comes in here. I twist my head away but the girl grasps my chin and pulls me to face her. I scrunch my eyelids shut, but it's too late. She's already seen enough. She pulls my face closer. I can feel her breath on my skin.

"How did that happen?" she asks. "One's gray and the other's—"

"Green. I know." I open my eyes a tiny crack and watch her through slitted lids.

She punches me in the shoulder playfully. "Don't be embarrassed. I'd *pay* for eyes like that. How did they get that way?"

"I don't know." It's true, but will she believe me? Realizing there's no point in hiding them anymore, I open my eyes.

"Are we in the lockup?" I ask her.

"Good one!" She slaps my back as if I've made a joke, the motion releasing another barrage of coughing.

When I recover, I try again. "No, seriously. I seem to be having trouble remembering how I got here." Actually, I'm having trouble remembering much of anything. It's as if I left my quarters this morning, passed out, and woke up here. Wherever *here* is. I pull the blankets tight around me.

"The Med-Techs brought you." The girl pats my ankle through the covers. "You were asleep, which I thought was weird. I mean, most girls are excited to be here, but you were out like a light."

"Most girls? What are you talking about? Where are we?"

"The Nest, of course."

"The Nest?" I sit bolt upright, shoving her aside. "*This* is the Nest?" I gaze around the cramped space trying to make sense of it. That can't be right. Whatever tricks my memory is playing, there's no way I'm supposed to be in the *Nest*.

"Where did you think you were?" she asks, indicating her swollen belly. She's an Expectant, but she seems so young, even younger than me. I know that some girls discover motherhood as their Calling pretty early, but she's only a child herself. "You didn't really think we were in the lockup, did you? Why on earth would you think that? Why would they put a bunch of Expectants in the lockup?"

"This is a mistake," I insist.

"Did you have a bad Procedure? Is that what's upsetting you?"

"I didn't *have* the Procedure." I run my fingers along my flat belly to convince myself.

"Maybe you blotted it out. Repressed it." She stumbles over the word.

I draw my wrists to my temples and am assaulted by a pain in my right arm. I jerk up my sleeve to reveal a neat dressing, taped securely over my arm, the blue and purple edges of a bruise blossoming around it. I press it experimentally. It throbs in response. It can't be more than a day old. I probe the skin around it with my fingertips. It's a real injury, even though I have no recollection of how it happened. But if there's one thing I know about the Nest, it's that no one gets hurt here. That's its purpose. To keep all Expectants safe and sound. To protect the next generation of our dwindling population. I couldn't have been here when this happened

Then, I notice something else: My communicator is missing. I check both wrists, and the pockets of the robe before scanning the surface of the bedside table. It's nowhere. I look at the other girl's wrists. Her communicator is right where it should be.

"Where's my communicator?" I ask her.

She looks around, opening and shutting a drawer in the night-stand that I had failed to notice. Empty.

"That's odd," she says. "I guess you didn't have one when they brought you. Where did you see it last?"

I try to remember, but my mind is a blank. "I don't know."

"Seriously? Amnesia?" Ace's voice has lost none of its cheer-iness. "That's great! A mystery to solve! It gets so boring in here sometimes."

I run my thumb and forefinger over my brow, trying to remember anything. An image of a woman in white scrubs flickers into my mind. A Med-Tech? Ace perches beside me on the bed, her toe tracing circles in the carpet. I force myself to stand up, recoiling when my leg gives out. I half-sit, half-stumble back on to the cot. Raising my hem, I'm shocked to discover a thick elastic brace over an obviously swollen knee. I raise an eyebrow and glare at Ace. "This didn't happen in the Nest, did it?"

She bends down to examine it.

"Maybe we should call someone?" I indicate her communi-cator. Her eyes widen for a moment, and she swallows before nodding and pressing the button to open a comm-channel. Nothing happens. She looks away.

"Sorry. I guess it needs a recharge," she says. When she doesn't speak again, I wrap my fingers around the bedframe and hoist myself up, holding tight until I manage to balance on my injured leg. Ignoring the heavy feeling in my limbs, I shuffle to the door and press the panel beside it. Nothing happens. I whirl on Ace. "This doesn't seem to be working either. Why?"

She bounds over to me. The movement looks almost comical given the size of her belly. She gathers my good arm in hers to pull me back to the cot, murmuring in soothing tones, "I'm sure it's only a glitch. Someone will come soon to check on us. They always do."

She arranges me on the edge of the mattress and sits beside me, fidgeting with the fringe of a blanket. Beads of sweat form on my forehead, and I start to feel dizzy. I press my fingers to my temples. "I don't understand what's happening."

"We'll figure it out. Try to relax."

Her words frighten me. *Why?* The blanket falls to the floor and puddles at her feet. "Why did you say that?"

"You seemed upset," she says. "I just thought you should relax. Then your memory might come back on its own. Maybe do some breathing exercises or something."

That word. *Relax*. Why does it bother me? Pushing to my feet again I'm pleased that I manage to avoid most of the pain by knowing how to balance on my good leg. I start pacing in the cramped space between the cots with a pronounced limp but steady enough. Ace nudges the blanket aside, so I don't trip over it. My legs don't feel so heavy anymore. The movement is helping. Fragments of what feel like memories start slotting into place. They don't make sense at first.

"I think I went to the Clinic. Yes, I'm sure that's right. A Med-Tech took me to a room," I mutter to myself. "Her name was Rho and she wanted to know why I asked for … Delta?" I glance at Ace whose skin is now pale. She remains on the edge of the cot, her fingers wrapped around the metal frame. I focus back into my memories. Fragments are returning. A setting sun. A pool of water. Two scampering squirrels. A scrap of crimson fabric with shiny gold thread. My arm twinges. I touch my fingertips to my eyelids, but the memories slip away. Whatever happened, the one thing that makes the least sense is…

"Why did they bring me here?" I say more to myself than the other girl.

"There's only one reason anyone is brought here." Ace bends to retrieve the blanket and starts to fold it into neat squares before pressing it to her chest.

"That doesn't make any sense. I told you, I haven't had the Procedure."

"There is technically *one* other way." Ace is gripping the blanket so tight her knuckles are turning white. "You know how it used to happen, in the days before the palisade, right? With the"—her voice turns to a hushed whisper—"*demen*?"

That word is all I need to break through the logjam in my mind.

Everything comes rushing back. I collapse on to the second cot, staring straight ahead as the memories flood in. The *deman* leaping out of the tree outside the Clinic. Patching me up. Then that Med-Tech. Rho Zee. I was supposed to deliver a message. To Delta.

I start to shake as Ace waves her hand in front of me. "Omega?"

Before I can respond, the door opens to reveal a figure in a long black coat and silver buttons: a Protector. Ace stumbles across the room.

"Omega Wye?" the Protector's voice booms into the silence. "I'm Commander Theta. Come with me please." She strides into the room and I back away. Crawling over the mattress, I press myself against the wall, as far away from her as physically possible.

"A little help?" She directs her words into the hallway. Two Med-Techs appear behind her. One is short with dark skin and thick black hair swept back in a white headband. The other is taller with short copper-tinged hair and cornflower blue eyes. Despite the differences in their heights, they move in unison, forming a human wall in front of me.

"Come along now. We won't hurt you," the copper-haired one says as they both reach for me. Their hands are like extended claws, coming in for the kill. This is supposed to be a safe place, but I've never felt more scared.

I press my entire body into the wall, ignoring the pain in my injuries. The plaster is hard and cold against my back. "Wait," I say. "There's been a mistake." Ignoring my words, the taller woman grasps my good arm and beckons to her partner who glances at me, trembling as she retrieves a syringe from her pocket. She gasps when she sees my eyes. I guess no one warned her about them.

"No! Don't!" Ace cries out as the needle pierces my skin.

"Don't worry. It's only a muscle relaxant. It won't hurt her." The dark Med-Tech attempts to reassure Ace, but her fingers are trembling against my arm while her partner maintains the unbreakable hold on my shoulder. Gradually, my body goes limp. I slide down the wall, and the Med-Techs gather me up between them. They carry me to the hallway and deposit me in a waiting wheelchair.

As the door shuts behind us, I hear Ace's muffled cry. "Try and cooperate with them, Omega. They might let you keep the baby."

The drug has taken effect now. I can see and hear everything, but I can't move, as the Med-Techs wheel me down the corridor in a procession with the commander at the helm, the tall Med-Tech directly behind her, and the other woman behind me, pushing the chair. Her warm breaths puff down the back of my neck. We seem to be traveling a long way. The corridors become dimmer and quieter. The few women we pass turn their heads and scurry away. The sound of the commander's boot heels clacking against the tiled floor is almost deafening.

"Should we be doing this?" the Med-Tech behind me whispers to her colleague who has dropped back a few paces and is now within earshot. She doesn't respond. She's watching the commander's back intently. The Protector's strides are brisk, her long coat flapping against her thighs as she strides forward. The Med-Tech speaks again, even more quietly. "This is a restricted area. We shouldn't be here."

The commander stops, indicating a recessed doorway directly in front of her. The Med-Techs follow suit, and the wheelchair grinds to a halt. "Open it," the commander says. Without missing a beat, the taller Med-Tech swipes her communicator along the panel. A green light flashes as the door slides open. "Take her inside."

The chair moves forward and we are inside the dark room. The air is stale.

"Lights," the commander says.

There's a buzzing sound as the room is illuminated by harsh light. It looks like a disused birthing room. An old-fashioned maternity bed with uncomfortable looking metal stirrups takes up its center. I recognize it from the medical history texts. Sagging laminated benches line the walls. The three women remain behind me. I feel something warm against my shoulder. A reassuring hand?

"Turn her," the commander says, her voice sharp as steel. The chair rotates, and I am facing her again. Her expression is a mask of cool efficiency, matching her tailored jacket with its shining buttons. My limbs begin to jerk, causing the metal struts of the chair to rattle. The commander swears under her breath. "It's wearing off. Secure her." She passes a set of restraints to the copper-haired Med-Tech. Thin plastic bands encircle my wrists and ankles as the Med-Tech obeys her orders and ties me to the chair. The plastic bites into my flesh. My injured limbs scream in protest.

The commander's voice slices the air. "You're all mine now, Daughter Wye."

Momentarily, I feel that brief warmth at the back of my neck where the commander won't see. It's definitely a hand pressing against me.

"Leave us," the commander says. The comforting touch disappears from my shoulder. Without a word, the two Med-Techs retreat to the door. "And lock the door on the way out." It closes behind them and the room reverberates with the sound of the lock clicking into place.

We're all alone.

Chapter 6

My wrists and ankles burn from the restraints, but the pain is nothing compared to my fear. The Protector stares directly into my eyes. *My real eyes.* She inhales and mutters something under her breath. Then she strides to the far wall and drags a chair directly in front of me, scraping its metal legs across the linoleum. Sitting stiff and straight, she adjusts her jacket. Even seated, she's so tall I have to crane my neck to face her. The woman doesn't speak, just stares and stares. I wish I could melt into the floor. I turn my face down to avoid her gaze, but she grabs my chin hard between her thumb and forefinger and jerks, clutching me like a vice, forcing me to look at her.

"Don't be so coy, Daughter Wye." She releases her grip and I recoil, slamming my back against the struts of the wheelchair. I don't know what I expect her to do next, but it isn't what she actually does. Slowly, as if in a trance, she lifts her fingertips to my cheek. "Remarkable," she whispers, swallowing hard before she blinks and pushes to her feet, shoving her chair so hard it clangs to the floor. "Man-lovers, both of you. No better than *demen* yourselves."

This woman is dangerous and clearly unhinged. She could kill me and no one would ever know. By the time my mother resurfaces, I could already be dead. Or worse. The Protector is hovering over me, glowering. Her fingers tighten around the arms of the wheelchair. Then, quietly, deliberately, she straightens up and removes something from her jacket pocket. It's a wadded bundle of dark cloth. She snaps her wrist and the bundle unfurls. It's a thin strip of dark crimson fabric shot through with fine gold thread. "Recognize this?"

My expression must give me away.

"Yes, I thought so." Moving in closer, she lifts the bandage in front of me and leans over my shoulder, tying it into a makeshift blindfold. The scent of bitter lemon wafts over me. She's wearing some kind of citrus fragrance. "I don't need to look into your sad little monster's eyes for this." Her hot breath puffs against my cheek as she fastens the knot behind my head. She moves away and I hear her chair scrape against the floor as she retrieves it. When she speaks again, her voice is very close. Directly in front of me. "So, Daughter Wye, what shall we talk about?"

It's not only my eyes. She knows about the *deman* too. That Med-Tech, Rho Zee, must have reported me. The whole scene with Ace was a set-up to get me talking. Do they think I'm mixed up with Delta, and that monster outside? The commander remains silent, the air thick with menace. I have to say something.

"What do you want to know?" I'm surprised at how steady I manage to sound.

"What do you think?"

"*Demen*?"

"I knew you weren't as stupid as you look. Why don't we have a nice little chat about your boyfriend?"

"My what?"

"Your little friend, the one hiding around the Clinic."

"He's not my friend. I just ran into him."

"Really? Why do I have trouble believing that?"

"It's the truth." I flex my fingers and the plastic ties bite into my skin. Sucking my lower lip between my teeth, I stifle a cry.

"The apple really doesn't fall far from the tree, does it? Tell me where he is." Her voice is closer, louder. I cower but don't have much room for movement.

"I don't know. He was outside the Clinic, but he left."

Without any warning her hand is around my throat. She's not gripping hard enough to cut off my air, but the threat is clearly there. The lemon scent strengthens as I wrap my fingers around the arms of the chair, ignoring the sting of the plastic ties.

"We know you're working with him," the commander says.

"He's not in Delta's quarters. *Where is he*?" Her grip relaxes as if to coax me to answer.

"I don't know. I don't know. I don't know." I repeat it like a mantra, hoping it will satisfy her.

"Sounds like you don't know much. Perhaps this interview is over?" The threat in her voice is unmistakable. Her chair slides away and I exhale in relief until a blade presses against my throat and the Protector's hot breath assaults my skin. I try not to move, not even to swallow. Then I hear the door slide open.

"Commander Theta?" It's a stranger's voice, low and authoritative, coming from the hallway. Then complete silence. The blade disappears from my neck.

"Yes, ma'am?" The commander's voice is calmer now, official.

"What are you doing?" the stranger continues.

"Interrogating this criminal."

"Criminal?"

"She's been consorting with a *deman*. She admits it herself."

"So I've heard." The woman sounds old. Her voice cracks when she speaks.

"There could be more of them. *She* could be carrying his child!" The commander sounds like she's losing control again.

"Unlikely, Commander."

"But, Ma'am—"

"Her test was negative, Theta." The stranger's voice has softened, taking on a motherly cadence, as if berating a child. She reminds me of someone, but I can't think who.

"That means nothing," the commander says. "She was with him tonight. A positive result may take weeks."

"Ma'am, if I may." A third voice sounds from the hallway. I recognize it as the Med-Tech who pushed the wheelchair earlier and tried to comfort me. "We should keep the girl safe in the Nest. Until we know for sure."

"Commander." I discern a hint of warning in the older voice, but the warning comes too late. A powerful blow connects with my stomach, winding me. I gasp for air, tears pouring down my cheeks, as I attempt to untangle the din of voices.

"Remove her," the older woman says.

Commander Theta hisses into my ear. "It's for your own good. You're better off without his baby. Believe me, I know." A scuffle ensues, and the commander's voice is defiant now. "Don't bother. I'm leaving." As the door closes, she calls out, "Don't let her fool you, ma'am. She's just like her mother."

Hurried footsteps approach and I feel a pair of gentle arms wrap around my shoulders. A hand rubs my back. The Med-Tech? I hiccup back tears of relief as she mutters soothing words.

"Why does the commander think I'm an Expectant?" My question comes out as a sob.

"It's very unlikely you are an Expectant, and even more unlikely she could hurt the child that way if you were. But she will be counseled with respect to her actions here today." The older voice is closer now too.

The Med-Tech is working on my blindfold. It's soaked through with my tears. When she removes it, an old woman is peering at me from a few paces away. She has leathery olive skin and deep green eyes, pale with age. Her hair is thick and gray. It cascades over her shoulders in wiry strands. She's wearing long dark robes, belted loose at her waist with a crimson tie, and she's hunched over a gnarled wooden cane.

It can't be.

"Are you…?" I'm unable to complete the sentence.

"Yes, child. I am an Elder." She notices the bindings on my wrists. Despite her stooped posture, she takes a few steps forward with the assistance of her cane. Then she leans down to place a wrinkled hand on one of mine before addressing the Med-Tech. "Healer, can you do something about these?"

Without a word, the Med-Tech races to the counter and jerks open random drawers and cabinets until she finds an emergency kit. Prying it open, she extracts a pair of scissors and crouches in front of me to attack the bindings. I fix my attention on the Elder.

"Remarkable." She echoes the commander's earlier words when she looks into my eyes.

"My mother says it's a genetic anomaly," I say. "Nothing to worry about."

"I know," she says.

Taking a slow and painful-looking step back, she leans heavily on her cane. Although her words are formal, the hint of a smile plays over her features. "Omega Wye, daughter of Sigma." Her voice cracks on my mother's name. "You may call me Omicron."

If the Elders are involved, this is serious. Of course it's serious. A *deman* is inside the palisade. The Elders have to be here. They don't involve themselves in our day-to-day governance. They simply watch and advise. But they do become active if something serious happens, like that flood at the factory or the fire in the south fields last harvest season. They help coordinate the planning and relief efforts and provide support and counsel where they can.

"I understand you have encountered a man, within our walls," she says.

Finally free of my bonds, I slump forward, almost toppling from the chair. The Med-Tech steadies me, looking to the Elder for guidance. Omicron indicates the birthing bed with the tip of her cane. The Med-Tech loops my arm over her shoulder and hoists me across the room, depositing me on its padded surface. The pain from the commander's blow is subsiding, but I feel weak and tired, and very confused. Now that my wrists and ankles are free, the throbbing from my other injuries seems to have lessened. Maybe I'm going into shock.

The Med-Tech adjusts the back support, enabling me to recline into a more comfortable position. As she did earlier, she places her hand on my shoulder. It's so reassuring that I want to forget about everything and melt into her. Wrestling with her cane, Omicron drags the metal chair to the side of the bed. The Med-

Tech leaps up to assist her, but the older woman waves her away. As she deposits herself awkwardly beside me, I smell fresh gardenias.

"You never encountered any men before today?" she asks.

"No." My voice is steadier now.

"What did he want?"

"He asked me to give a message to—"

"Delta?"

I'm suddenly suspicious. Is this another trap?

As if reading my thoughts, the Elder says, "This must be very confusing for you. You probably have some questions for me." The corners of her mouth droop and I notice the wrinkles etched around them. "Please. Ask me anything. It is important that we trust each other."

I hesitate, then realizing I have nothing to lose, I say, "So *demen* aren't extinct?"

"It would appear not."

"The one I met, he didn't actually hurt me."

The Elder follows my gaze toward the bandage on the counter, the one the *deman* made for me. She props her cane against her knees. "He may not be dangerous."

I run my fingers down my flat belly, thinking about when I was in the Nest. "I had an Expectancy test?"

"While you were asleep." The Med-Tech rests her palm on the back of the birthing bed.

"Commander Theta didn't believe this man would have let you alone without, well, I'm sure you can guess what she feared," Omicron says.

"She told me. She thought I was *with* him. Why would she think that?" The *deman's* face flashes through my mind, dirty and hairy, one lip imperfectly curving higher than the other.

"The commander has her reasons," Omicron says. Her forehead creases more deeply.

I prop myself higher and notice a silent communication pass

between Omicron and the Med-Tech. "You say you were not *intimate* with this boy?" the Elder asks, raising a silvered brow.

"Intimate? No, of course not." I try to maneuver my legs over the edge of the bed, but she's in my way. "And you said the test was negative."

"It's not us, child." The Med-Tech's voice is low against my ear. "It's Commander Theta. She'll insist there's a risk of Expectancy because she knows you had contact with him. The tests are not one hundred percent accurate, particularly if your contact with this man was very recent. Technically, she can insist you remain detained in the Nest until we're sure."

Omicron looks me over. "I'm assuming you would rather return to your quarters if you had the choice?" She raises her brow again, a glimmer of a smile passing across her face.

The Med-Tech opens her mouth as if to speak, but the Elder quiets her with a gesture. "Don't worry, Healer. I will take care of it." She returns her attention to me and says, "Your mother is away." It's not a question.

She knots her fingers under her chin, her cane still resting on her knees. "Omega, I can return you to your quarters." My shoulders sag with relief. "But you will have to stay there until your mother returns. I will attempt to get word to her."

She stands with difficulty using her cane for leverage. "I'm afraid we have not seen the end of this matter. There is a man – or at least a boy – inside the walls. Too many people are aware of it, including Commander Theta."

"Unfortunately," the Med-Tech mutters under her breath, and the Elder shoots a warning glanceat her.

Omicron pats my good knee. "But the least we can do is get you home, my child. You've been through enough. For today."

Chapter 7

Omicron stands in the hallway outside the open door to the birthing room, speaking in hushed tones into a communicator. She hasn't answered any more of my questions but has reassured me several times that I'll be safe until my mother returns. The Med-Tech, whose name is Pi, has located a pair of coveralls for me to wear. She helps me replace the Nest-issued robe with the new gear, deftly avoiding my injuries. As I push my feet into the slippers she found for me, I try to avoid thinking about how many other people have worn them. They look like they might have been pale blue once, but now they're a dull gray. I've tried probing Pi for more information about what's going on, but she either doesn't know or won't tell me.

The heavy clack of a Protector's boots sounds from the hallway.

"Elder." Outside the door, a new voice greets Omicron. *Not Theta.*

"Thank you for coming," Omicron says, as she ushers a smartly dressed young Protector into the room. The woman is much shorter than Commander Theta, not much taller than me. Almost too short to be a Protector. They've had to relax the standards as the population thins. The woman stands to attention beside the Elder, white blonde hair framing her face. Omicron looks weary as she bends over her cane.

"Omega, this is Private Upsilon," the Elder says. "She will escort you to your quarters."

Upsilon takes a step toward me and then freezes when she gets her first good look at my eyes. Omicron pats her arm and the Protector relaxes her posture before speaking.

"Pleased to meet you, Daughter Wye." She stretches out a hand and I step forward to take it. Her grip is firm but not intimidating.

"Call me Omega." Even though "Daughter Wye" is my formal title, I've always hated the sound of it.

She turns her attention to Omicron. "I'll take her out the side entrance. I have a vehicle stationed there."

"Omega, I am sorry for what you have been through. Please try not to worry about Commander Theta. I know it's difficult for you to understand, but she means well. Sometimes her methods are unfortunate."

"Will she come back for me?"

Omicron's brow furrows. "Try not to worry, child. I will counsel the commander about her behavior, and we'll take other precautions. You will be safe."

She nods toward Upsilon who offers her a small salute. "Come, Daughter Wye ... Omega." She beckons toward the open doorway and moves aside for me to pass.

As I head for the door, Omicron says, "It was a pleasure to finally meet you, Omega. I'm sorry it could not have been under more pleasant circumstances." She, too, steps aside as the Protector leads me forward. I turn to say goodbye, but the Elder and Med-Tech are now huddled in a low, urgent conversation.

Private Upsilon directs me through a dimly lit hallway. I follow a few paces behind her, occasionally tripping over my feet in the unfamiliar slippers as I work the stiffness from my sore knee. The Protector doesn't seem to mind my lagging pace. This passageway seems completely abandoned. It's dusty and there's no sign of life anywhere. We continue walking for what seems like a long time. Finally, Upsilon stops and waves her communicator over a keypad mounted on the wall. A panel beside it slides open to reveal a set of steps leading down to a patch of gravel overgrown with weeds. A small vehicle is parked there. Upsilon guides me out, closing the panel behind us. She flicks a button on her communicator and the headlights flash on either side of the vehicle as the doors swing open.

"Ever been in one of these?" She runs a hand over the hood.

"No." I've never been in any kind of transport. I walk everywhere except when my mother lets me borrow her pushbike for the occasional run to the market.

Upsilon ushers me to the passenger side door. Lowering myself into the seat, I watch her slip gracefully into the driver's space opposite. There's a large steering wheel and a control panel on her side. She reaches behind her and pulls a wide belt over her left shoulder, snapping it into place at her right thigh. She turns to me.

"Seat belt," she says. I realize I'm supposed to do the same. I crane my neck over my left shoulder, but don't see anything. "Other side." She points to the hook over my right shoulder. My cheeks flush as I grab for the belt.

She swipes her communicator over the control panel, and the vehicle hums to life. We lurch backward, but my seatbelt catches me, causing an ache in my stomach. She turns the wheel and the car circles out of the lot and makes its way to the main causeway. It's late afternoon. The route is empty other than some young mothers pushing infants in strollers. Watching them, it's easy to see the attraction of motherhood as a Calling. They seem so happy and relaxed. One woman cradles a newborn in her arms as a second woman leans over and presses a kiss to her forehead.

A family.

A pang of loneliness stabs through me.

"What time is it?" I ask Upsilon, who's humming an unfamiliar tune.

"First shift after lunch."

"What day?"

"Since you've been in the Nest? Only overnight. It probably seems longer." She shoots me a meaningful glance. Peering through the tinted windows, I realize how fast we're moving. Faster than Mom's pushbike, that's for sure. We pass the sprawling grounds that separate the Nest from the Clinic, and move on to the wider transit path. The sun beats against my cheek through the tinted window. Untidy patches of flowers are dotted around solar lamps and community benches. We pass a few workers on pushbikes heading back from their shifts at the factories and farms. I can tell from their uniforms where they work.

"You were probably expecting something faster," Upsilon says. "These electric cars are nowhere near as powerful as the old gas guzzlers, but they get us from Alpha to Beta."

Gas-guzzlers? I remember the term from history class. The *demen* used them as part of their systematic degradation of the planet before the palisade was built to keep out the pollution. And the polluters. No way was I expecting a gas-guzzler. We drive on in silence. I think I dozed off because I'm startled by the sound of the Protector's voice as the vehicle grinds to a stop by the side door of the housing block.

"Home sweet home," she says. Usually only bicycles are kept here. Even though the lot is empty now, there's barely enough room for the vehicle. It's weird to think it was only yesterday I walked out the front entrance of this cinderblock building for my shift at the factory. This structure is roughly the same size as the factory, but is divided into six floors rather than the two levels in the plant. The lower floors of the housing block comprise the smaller more basic living spaces while the upper floors house more lavish dwellings.

Upsilon whisks her communicator over the panel to shut off the engine. We both get out of the vehicle at the same time and she motions me toward the side door, following close behind. She's keeping watch.

I raise my wrist to the panel, forgetting that my communicator is gone. Upsilon moves past me and opens the door with her own device. "Don't worry. We'll arrange for a new communicator as soon as we can."

I follow her down the corridor. She knows exactly where to go. When we arrive at my door, she presses the buzzer. When there's no answer, Upsilon uses her emergency override code to get in.

Inside the dwelling, she flicks on the lights. The space is empty. The tiny living-room-slash-kitchen seems a little smaller without Mom pottering around. The bright yellow paint she used to make the place more cheery when I was a child is now peeling. She was so proud when she first painted it. It had been my color choice. I was only about two hundred weeks old at the time. Probably we couldn't easily get our hands on that much decorative paint anymore if we wanted to redo it.

Upsilon indicates one of our shabby living rooms chairs. "Why don't you sit for a while? I'll get you some water." She heads for the kitchen.

"Are you staying?" I don't know how I feel about having a Protector stationed in my quarters, even a relatively nice one.

"No. I have a few things to take care of. Omicron asked me to get you settled and come back to check on you later. You'll need to keep the door locked." Upsilon rinses a mug and fills it with water before pressing it into my hand. "I'll leave an emergency signal device with you." She fumbles for something in her pocket and retrieves a small metal object that she passes to me. It's no bigger than my thumbnail. The metal is cool to the touch. The device emits a faint pulse. "It's a direct line to my communicator," she explains. "If you need me, just wave it over the wall screen and it will buzz me." She points to the data-port on our living room wall. "Will you be alright for now?"

I muster the best smile I can. She turns to the door. Before exiting she says, "Don't hesitate to use the signal if you need me. I'll be back to check on you at"—she glances at her communicator—"eighteen hundred hours."

She offers me a small salute as she exits. The door locks behind her. I let out a breath I didn't realize I was holding and drop the signal device into the pocket of my borrowed coveralls. I realize I want them off. Now. I want all reminders of what I've been through gone. I only hope I'm safe enough with Upsilon's security measures in place. I head for the bathroom and make sure I lock the door behind me.

Chapter 8

I can't stop shivering despite the steaming shower. I tell myself I'm safe now. I'm home. Everything's going to be alright. Dull pain radiates from my abdomen as the water flows over my stomach. There's a sizeable bruise, beginning to turn crimson around the edges, where the commander hit me. I've let my injured arm get wet so I shake it out, hoping it won't need another dressing. The brace on my knee didn't fare so well. I couldn't keep it dry so I had to remove the bandage. It doesn't look too bad. A little swollen but it's bearing my weight better.

The buzzer at the front door sounds. It can't be Mom. She wouldn't ring the bell, and it's too early for Upsilon to have returned. I shut off the water and shiver as I grab for my pajamas. Whoever is outside is now holding the button down causing a continuous ringing that's hurting my ears. I throw my robe over my pajamas and belt it at the waist before finger combing my wet hair, leaving untidy clumps hanging around my shoulders. Rattled by the noise, I head for the door where the buzzing is suddenly replaced by an urgent knocking. I dash to the intercom and press the button. "Who is it?"

"It's Gamma. Are you okay?" She sounds frantic. Of course. I was supposed to meet her for dinner yesterday. The panel shudders as she pummels the door from the outside. Without thinking it through, I open it. She stands on the threshold, arms braced against the doorjamb, breathing heavily. She's still in her factory uniform. "I've been ringing and ringing. What's going on?"

"I was in the shower." I indicate my damp hair, draped messily around my face.

She pushes past me and strides inside. "How could you not call me? I thought something had happened when I didn't hear from you last night and then you weren't on shift this morning.

And now I find you lounging around in your PJs."

I move forward, hands raised in surrender.

That's when she notices.

My eyes.

The frozen look of disbelief on her face is all I need to remind me that I forgot to look for my spare contacts before my shower.

Her mouth drops open.

"It's only a birth defect. It's no big deal," I say.

"They've always been this way?" she asks.

"Yes."

"And you never thought to tell me? Your best friend? What else haven't you told me? How about where you really were last night? You weren't in the Clinic. I checked my mom's datapad."

"It's kind of a long story."

"That's what they all say. I thought you were better than that. I thought we were friends."

"We are, but—"

"Save it." She turns on her heel and storms out.

I trail after her, but I'm much slower in my bare feet, and I need to stop to fix the door so it doesn't lock behind me. I have no way of opening it again without my communicator. And part of me thinks it's safer to let Gamma stew in her own juices. I've seen her get like this before, but never with me. I know I can't really leave her this way.

The fire door slams at the end of the corridor. She's obviously avoiding the less-than-reliable elevator. When I get to the bottom of the stairwell, she's at least a flight above me. I can hear her stomping footsteps further up the stairs. She's heading up to her quarters. I stumble over the hem of my robe and curse as I grab at the twisted metal banister to right myself. By the time I reach the sixth floor, there's no sign of her. I head for her door and knock loudly, not caring that I'm on the important folks' floor in a bathrobe without my contacts.

When Gamma's door opens, I find myself face to face with her mother, Ma Temple. Gamma's mom is an anomaly because she has a dual Calling: motherhood and Med-Tech. It's rare, but it happens. Of the two, motherhood is the higher vocation, attracting the honorific "Ma" title like my own mom. She examines me from head to toe, not flinching at my appearance, or my eyes. Rather, she steps aside and motions me in.

"I suppose we'd better get that daughter of mine back here and sort this out," she says.

Ma Temple is so much more stylish than my own mother, with her scarlet tunic over fitted slacks. The combination works somehow despite her pale complexion. She leads me to the lounge suite that takes pride of place in the living area and gestures for me to sit.

A door cracks open behind her to reveal Gamma hovering just inside the kitchen, scowling.

Ma Temple addresses her. "Could you come in here please?"

Gamma takes a reluctant step, glaring at me.

"I suppose this"—Ma Temple indicates my eyes—"explains this." Now she's pointing at her daughter. I want to be angry with Gamma, but it's true that I've kept this hidden from her our whole lives. It's not every day you find out your best friend is concealing an inexplicable mutation.

Gamma looks from her mother to me and back again.

"You know about this?" Gamma says to her mom.

Ma Temple doesn't deny it. My back stiffens. She's obviously been keeping some secrets of her own. She beckons us to the sofa. This time I allow myself to sit. The cushions are so plush, I sink into them despite my best efforts to sit up straight.

"I suppose I owe you both an explanation," Ma Temple says. "I only wish your mother were here, Omega. I told her something like this would happen. I'm surprised it didn't happen sooner."

My fingers beat a tattoo on the armrest. Gamma's jaw sets into a tight line. Ma Temple touches her arm gently. "Honey, why don't you come with me to the kitchen? We can calm down and maybe fix some hot chocolate? Then we can sit and talk."

Hot chocolate. Ma Temple's answer for everything. It usually works on Gamma. I want to push Ma Temple to start talking now, but that won't be possible until Gamma gets her temper under control.

"Omega, you'll be alright here for a few moments on your own, won't you?" Ma Temple clearly isn't expecting a response.

They're in the kitchen for a long time. Their voices rise in pitch until the kettle whistles. Then the smell of hot chocolate wafts into the living room. It causes me to salivate, despite the charged atmosphere. I haven't eaten anything since the factory yesterday.

Glancing out the picture window, I notice a hummingbird flitting around the branch of an oak tree. Quite a contrast to the view from the window in our quarters, overlooking the dumpster. The arguing from the kitchen has stopped. Gamma and Ma Temple return. Ma Temple holds two steaming mugs while Gamma cradles the third to her chest. Ma Temple presses one of her mugs to Gamma who takes it automatically. "Honey, why don't you give this to your friend?" She emphasizes the last word and Gamma groans.

My heart sinks as I remember Gamma at the factory. Have I lost her as a friend? After a few moments, she places the extra mug on the coffee table in front of me and shuffles away with her own. She stops when she realizes her mother has taken the chair across from me, and the only place left for her to sit is on the sofa beside me.

I pull my legs aside so Gamma can pass without having to touch me. She gets like this when she's annoyed even though she's never been this angry with me before. Maybe she's scared of me now, of what my eyes might really mean.

"Gamma, please," I say. "I should've told you sooner, but it doesn't change who I am."

She still won't look at me, and seems to be making sure she's sitting as far away as possible without leaving the sofa.

"Please, Ma Temple." I force myself to ignore Gamma. "Tell us."

Chapter 9

Ma Temple blows the steam from her mug before taking a deep draft and licking the residue from her top lip. Gamma curls her knees to her chest and hunches into the far corner of the sofa. Her mug is clasped between her fingers, but she isn't drinking. She's staring straight ahead and ignoring me. My hot chocolate doesn't seem so tantalizing anymore.

"What has your mother told you so far?" Ma Temple asks me.

"Nothing."

"She never told you anything about where you came from?"

"She never talks about her Procedure if that's what you mean."

Gamma's honeysuckle fragrance mingles with the aroma of the hot chocolate, a heady combination.

Ma Temple addresses her next words to Gamma. "Honey, do you remember what I told you about why you should never go outside the palisade? Back when you were young?"

Gamma releases her knees from her chest before she answers. "You said the *demen* hordes are still out there, even though they're supposed to have died out."

They're definitely still out there. At least one of them.

"Do you remember the story about the woman who went outside, and what happened to her?" Ma Temple asks.

Gamma leans over to deposit her mug on the coffee table, placing her elbows on her knees to focus on her mother, effectively blocking me out. Something passes between the two of them. I can tell by Ma Temple's expression and the sudden hard set of Gamma's shoulders.

"Maybe you should share that story with Omega," Ma Temple says. Gamma turns hesitantly to face me, her skin pale. I have a bad feeling about this. If the story upsets Gamma so much, do I really want to hear it? A breeze blows a tree branch against the window, startling me. I reach for the table and accidentally bump my hot chocolate, causing it to drip over the mug and down one of the table legs. The sludge begins to soak into the white carpet.

Embarrassed, I glance at Ma Temple.

"Don't worry about it." Ma Temple stands. "I'll take care of it. Gamma, why don't you tell Omega what I told you?"

Gamma doesn't seem so angry anymore. If anything, she looks sad. Ma Temple goes to the kitchen so the two of us are alone now.

Gamma inches a little closer. "Can I see your eyes again?"

I turn to face her. She exhales loudly as she presses her fingertips on the tops of my cheekbones directly below my lower lids.

"How have you hidden them?"

"Contact lenses. Little pieces of plastic I use to cover them."

Gamma's lips form into a round "o". Then she asks, "Are they painful?"

"No, only if my eyes get dry. I'm used to it now." I pull further away. "What did your mother want you to tell me?"

She blinks and straightens. "Honestly, all my life I thought it was just a story Mom told me, to scare me out of ever thinking about trying to get outside the palisade. Remember how adventurous I was back then?"

The memories of her plans to do death-defying stunts flood back. I don't know why I ever thought I could be an explorer. She's the one with the adventurous streak.

"I don't know why I never figured it out before," she says. "I mean, that the story was true."

My hands begin to shake and I rest them against my knees.

"My mother used to tell me about a woman who had been Called to motherhood," Gamma says. "It was a while back. She was planning to have the Procedure but she couldn't go through with it. She was worried about the society inside the walls. Worried about the kind of world her child would grow up in. She didn't think we could sustain ourselves forever, and she wanted to go outside. To see if there was anything out there. People to trade with, to help us grow."

"Sounds like my mother," I start to say. The words die on my lips.

Gamma collects my hands between hers, pulling me forward. "This woman – she snuck outside the palisade. Only once. That's all it took."

It feels like a heavy weight has descended on my chest.

"She was attacked?" I say.

"She went missing for several days. Her partner was wild with fear. The Protectors were planning a search party, but it ended up not being necessary."

"Why not?" My voice sounds tinny in my ears.

"This woman, she had left her communicator behind. It looked as if she didn't want to be followed. But no one realized she had taken an emergency beacon with her. A few days after she disappeared, the signal was activated. From outside the palisade. The Protectors found her near the boundary, badly injured and unconscious with no memory of activating the signal. The Med-Techs assumed her memory had been affected by the trauma. Later, she was able to recall some of the things the *deman* did to her. Her physical injuries were healing, but the Med-Techs discovered something else." Gamma sinks back into the sofa, releasing my hands.

I barely hear Ma Temple enter the room. She walks over to us and pats my knee before wiping the spilled chocolate from the glass table and leaning over with a rag to mop up the stain on the carpet. When she's done, she perches on the arm of the sofa.

I speak more to myself than to anyone else. "So, that's why my eyes are like this?"

Ma Temple nods. "When a woman has the Procedure the Med-Techs can control for genetic abnormalities, but when a *deman*—"

"A *deman* did that to my mother. She never had the Procedure. Why didn't she tell me?"

"She was trying to protect you," Ma Temple says.

"How do you know all this?"

"Where do you think she gets the contact lenses?"

Gamma bolts forward, her voice rising in pitch. "You mean you've helped Ma Wye all this time? Helped her lie to Omega? And to me?"

"Honey, calm down."

Gamma stalks to the window, scaring away the hummingbird that has been hovering there. I can see clouds gathering in the distance. I wonder if the dry spell is going to break. Probably not. The rainclouds always appear on the horizon, but they never seem to get any closer. It's like they're taunting us.

Ma Temple raises her voice. "It started long before either of you were born. We didn't mean to hurt you. Either of you. I was on duty at the Clinic when they brought Ma Wye in from the outside. I examined her then, and worked on her later when we began to suspect that she might have become an Expectant."

Gamma is suddenly behind me. Her honeysuckle scent envelopes me. She reaches for my hand and our fingers interlace. Her skin is warm and soft. And reassuring. We're friends again.

"Maybe it was all meant to be," Ma Temple says. "After all, motherhood was her Calling."

Gamma's story is rattling around in my head when another thought strikes me. "How many people know about this?"

"Not many. There were only a few of us on duty that night and the Elders swore us to secrecy. Your mother managed to keep everything quiet even after she decided..." Ma Temple doesn't finish the sentence. She doesn't need to. I know what she was going to say.

"My mother was going to kill me," I say. I'm the one who shouldn't be here. I'm the monster. My lower lip quivers. "Why didn't she go through with it?"

Gamma's grip tightens around my hand.

"She came to talk to me before she decided. She asked me if anything was wrong with the baby, with you. She wanted to know if there was any chance you could be one of them."

"A *deman*," I whisper. Ma Temple regards me through lowered lashes. "She was going to kill me if I was a boy."

"But you weren't." Gamma interjects.

"Omega. Look at me." Ma Temple's voice is firm as she touches my knee and leans forward. She smells of hot chocolate. "Whatever else your mother may have done, she did it out of love. How you got here doesn't matter. She loves you. Think about it. She never had another daughter, did she? She spent her life caring for *you*."

"Despite what I am?"

"*Because* of what you are."

"So Mom finds out that I'm a girl, normal except for my eyes," I say.

"We had no way of knowing about that," Ma Temple says. "We can engineer the eye color in the embryo but not after the fetus is already growing. We didn't know until your eye color settled. Or rather colors. You were about forty weeks old. Your mother came to see me and we worked out the plan with the lenses. I've been helping her ever since."

"And the Elders know?" I ask.

"One does. We needed authorization to proceed with the birth. She permitted it out of sympathy to your mother and because she felt it was fated."

Omicron. It must be. That's why she wasn't surprised when she saw my eyes.

"Ma Temple?" I ask. "What happened to my mother's partner? Do you know?"

Gamma, who has remained by my side, reaches for what's left of my hot chocolate and presses the mug into my hand. I raise it to my lips but don't drink, waiting for Ma Temple's answer.

"She left your mother. Before you were born. When she couldn't talk her out of going through with it. I don't think they ever spoke again."

"What happened to her?"

"She devoted her life to protecting others from the threat of men. She never wanted anyone else to suffer your mother's fate. She loved her so much, you see. She joined the Protectorate and did quite well. She's a commander now."

It can't be.

A commander who hates my mother, accuses her of loving monsters, who can't bear to look at me. My voice cracks on my final question. I know what the answer will be, but I have to ask. "Do you remember her name?"

"I believe it was Theta."

My vision goes dark. This can't be happening. That woman, that commander was my mother's partner? It's my fault. I turned her into that wild animal that hurts the people she's supposed to protect, and my mother is out there with no idea. What if Theta goes looking for her?

"Omega?" Gamma is staring at me. "What is it?"

"Nothing," I stammer, depositing my mug on the table with a clink as I rise to my feet. "It's just a lot to take in."

"Of course it is," Ma Temple says as she stands beside me, concern blossoming across her face as she reaches for my elbow.

"I'm sorry. I have to process all this." I move to the door. I should get back to my quarters. Call Upsilon with that emergency signal. What if my mother comes back, and the Protectors are looking for her? What if Theta comes looking for me and finds me *here*? I'm putting the Temples in danger by being with them. Without my communicator there's no record I came in here, but might they have tracked Gamma's visit to my quarters?

"Wait." Gamma catches up to me. "Please, don't rush away."

"No!" My voice is harsher than I intend. "Truly, thank you

both. Thank you for telling me what I needed to know. Only I need some time. Please."

Ma Temple pulls her daughter back. "You need time to think it all through. I understand your mother is still away. You're welcome to stay here. We can give you some privacy."

I want to stay here, to tell them everything that's happened to me in the last few days, but I can't. There's no way I can drag my friends into this mess with Theta and that *deman*. It's too dangerous. Struggling to keep my voice level, I say, "I appreciate it so much, Ma Temple. You'll never understand how much, but I need to go."

Gamma breaks away from her mother and rushes over to hug me so tight it makes my bruises flare. I bite down on my lower lip. "Promise you'll call if you need to talk?"

"I promise."

"And if you don't call, I'll come looking for you."

I know she will, but I hope she doesn't. Not until I can talk to Upsilon. I can't guarantee Gamma will be safe with me. Not now.

Chapter 10

Unable to face the stairs, I chance the elevator. I jab my index finger over and over into the button for the ground floor. The grinding gears hurt my ears. The engineers should probably look at them as well. When the doors finally open at my landing, I shuffle out and head for my quarters. The door is still snibbed open, but the lights are off. Another power shortage? I press the panel but nothing happens. Maybe it's a blown fuse. Pulling the door closed, I head for the kitchen, arms outstretched against the darkness, to locate the emergency candles. The lock clicks behind me. I head back for the door wondering how that happened.

"Don't bother. I deactivated the lights and rigged the door." A disembodied voice rumbles from the living area. I whirl around barely able to make out the figure silhouetted against the sofa, bulky with squared shoulders.

The deman.

"It's only us, Daughter Wye," he says. His voice is deep and detached, hardly the way I remember it from the garden. He hasn't moved a muscle. If he hadn't spoken, I might have thought he was a mannequin placed there as a practical joke. The kind of thing Gamma might do as a prank. A flashlight blinds me. I try to avoid it, but the beam keeps moving, catching me full in the face.

"How do you know my name?"

"I almost had myself convinced I could trust you." He trains the light at my feet. "Why don't you have a seat, Daughter Wye? Right where you are. Back against the door please."

There's no option but to comply. I kneel by the door. He grunts as I curl my knees into my chest and wrap my arms around them. My thin cotton robe seems so flimsy.

Mustering what's left of my courage, I ask, "What do you want?" As my vision begins to adjust, I make out the planes of his face, jaw set hard, lips pressed into a thin line. He hasn't moved from the sofa. He raises the flashlight beam and shines it directly into my eyes.

"Could you please turn that off?" I try to inject some force into my words, but I'm exhausted by everything that's happened. If he's going to hurt me, I almost hope he'll do it quickly. I can't take much more of this. Between the commander's interrogation and the Temples' revelations, I'm done. "This would be easier if I could see you."

"Why?" he asks. "So you can give the Protectors a better description of me? No, Daughter Wye, I think you've seen enough."

"Please stop calling me that. And turn off the light."

"You really don't like being looked at, do you? I thought women were supposed to like being admired. That's what the history books say."

"Not by someone like you." Is there anyone who isn't going to attack me today? And what would a *deman* know about our history books?

"By a wild evil creature, you mean?" He doesn't try to conceal his sneer.

"You said it, not me. Why don't you prove you're better than that? Why don't you let me go? Or at least have the guts to turn on the lights. If you're going to hurt me, get on with it. Or get out."

My arms shiver around my knees, but I hold firm. The *deman* plays the light over my features. Then, without warning, he turns it off, plunging the room into darkness.

"Stay still," he says.

Determined to maintain some semblance of dignity, I try not to move. His measured breaths are still coming from across the room.

When he speaks again, his voice is unsteady, halting. "We made a deal, and you broke it."

"What?" I pull my robe tight around my legs.

"You sent them after me," he says. "I didn't think you'd do that. I let myself believe you'd keep your word."

"I didn't send them."

"How did they know where to look for me?" His voice is still coming from the sofa. He hasn't moved any closer.

I drop my head to my knees and brace my hands around the back of my neck. "My communicator, genius. They probably scanned for it." Then a sudden realization hits me. "The communicator. That's how you found out my name, where I live." He doesn't respond. "But how did you bypass the encryption?"

Demen are supposed to be brutes: more brawn than brain. How would he have learned to operate such a complex device? I risk a glance at him. Despite the darkness, I can make out his form, head bowed slightly forward.

"Don't get any ideas about using it to send a message. I dumped it. She probably has it by now.

"Who?"

"Your friend. That commander. Tall and dark. With the pissy attitude. She came looking for me, with some friends. I stayed hidden, but I heard them talking. When she couldn't find me, she decided to have another chat with you."

"When?"

"Not too long ago. Should be here soon."

What?

I twist around and hurl myself at the door, ignoring the pain in my arm, desperate to open it. It won't budge. He trains the light on me. What's the matter with him? Even if he doesn't care what she does to me, doesn't he realize what will happen if she catches him? I round on him, trying to keep my voice under control. "We have to get out of here. What do you think will happen if she finds us both here?"

"What do *you* think will happen?" He holds the flashlight vertically at his thigh. It illuminates his face as an eerie mask, his features uneven and threatening in the shadows.

"Please, think for a moment. Think about what you're doing." I don't know who scares me more: the *deman* in my living room, or that commander.

"If this is the only way I can find Delta, so be it. Either you agree to help me – really help me – or the Protectors can take us both."

"How can I help you? I'm in enough trouble as it is. Because of you." I have to press my palms into the solid panel behind me to stop myself from lunging at him. "Because of you she took me. They locked me up and interrogated me."

"That's why you spilled your guts to her?" He rises to his full height. I'd forgotten how big he is. I cower, but there's nowhere for me to go.

"I didn't have a choice. They took me. She hurt me." Tears of frustration blur my vision. We're going to end up back in Commander Theta's clutches and all because I can't get through to this brainless *deman*. He takes a step toward me and my legs go weak.

"I don't believe you," he says quietly. "She must have planted you outside the Clinic that night. Did they slash your arm to trick me, or did you do it to yourself?"

This is like talking to a rock. Despite my nerves screaming at me to stay put, I inch forward. He doesn't move, doesn't stop me. I keep moving closer, ignoring the stiffness in my legs. When I'm only a foot away, he steps to the side as if bracing for an attack. I don't give him the opportunity to react. I grab his hand, the one holding the flashlight, and guide the beam so it's level with my stomach. With my other hand, I pry open my robe and lift the bottom of my pajama shirt just enough for him to see the edges of the bruise where the commander punched me. "This is what that commander did to me. Because of you."

The *deman* leans in for a closer look. I can feel his breath tickle my skin, smell the hint of oak and lavender. I force myself to stay still.

He backs away, taking the light with him. "No. You're working with them."

"I'm not."

I'm desperate for him to believe me because I've worked out who scares me more, and it isn't him. I bend to retie the belt on my robe as the door rattles. He snaps off the light but not before I notice his panicked expression. There are voices outside and electronic beeps. Someone's working the lock. It must be the commander.

"Come here." He hisses at my ear before tugging me up on the sofa beside him. I stumble and groan at the pain in my arm. "Shh! Put your foot in my hands. I'm going to boost you."

"What?" I can't see anything. He grabs my bare foot and rests it in his palm. Then he interlaces his fingers beneath it.

"What are you doing?"

He shoves me upward. "Grab the edges."

I reach for the sides of the opening to the ventilation shaft above our heads. That must be how he came in. My arms burn, but I pull myself through as he pushes me from underneath. I have only just secured myself when he barrels into me and shoves me aside to slide something across the opening: the access panel. I hold my breath as the door opens below us. A light snaps on in my quarters, causing a dappled glow to spread into the vent through the metal grate the monster has fitted into place in the nick of time.

"We're in, Commander Theta."

The commander's here. With reinforcements.

Chapter 11

The *deman* wraps an arm around me from behind and clamps his hand over my mouth. I try to pull away. It's not as if I'm going to make a sound. He withdraws his hand, but stays close. It's fairly dark, but enough light is coming from below to make out his features. A muscle works in his jaw as he stares at the grate. The only thing visible beneath us is the sofa. The vent is grimy and smells of mildew.

"Check the bedrooms." The commander's order is followed by the sound of footsteps in the room underneath us. I can't tell how many people are down there, but they sound thorough. I can hear drawers being pulled from the dresser and cupboards opening and closing. The boy hasn't moved, hasn't looked at me again. His gaze is fixed on the grate. I want to get away from him, but I don't dare. The ventilation shaft is warm and cramped. I can't straighten my neck. He's hunched over to fit, but it doesn't seem to bother him.

"No one's here," someone says, followed by a string of curses in the commander's angry voice. I wonder what my mother could ever have seen in her. I lean in closer to the grate, pressing my ear to the metal.

"Orders, ma'am?" the commander's assistant asks.

"The girl was supposed to be here," Theta says.

I was meant to be safe from the commander in my quarters. Upsilon promised.

The *deman* boy grips my shoulders. I turn to glare at him, but he only holds a finger to his lips before letting go. The commander mutters under her breath. Then something smashes from the direction of the kitchen. I cringe, remembering the dishes draining beside the sink from the last meal I shared with Mom. I never cleared them away.

The commander's voice rings out, cold and officious. "Officer, there's nothing more for me to do here. The girl or her mother will return eventually. When they do, I want you to be waiting. Report in immediately."

"Yes, ma'am."

The door opens and closes, followed by the sound of a chair being dragged across the carpet, I think. The officer must be getting comfortable for the wait. I want to get back into my quarters. Apart from anything else, I need my spare lenses. Maybe we could overpower the guard. But she's probably armed. We wouldn't stand much of a chance. Could I count on this boy's help anyway? He taps my forearm, and I whirl around. He's so close I can almost feel his facial fur against my skin. I back away and raise my palms.

Placing an index finger to his lips, he points down the tunnel toward a muted light far ahead. He taps his chest, presumably to indicate that he will go first and I should follow. Then he presses his finger back to his lips. I roll my eyes, but he either ignores me or doesn't notice. Without a sound, he removes his shoes and places them to the side before angling past me in the confined space. I feel the heat of his body as he crawls past. Crouching on hands and knees, he starts half-crawling, half-sliding through the vent.

I press my ear to the grate once more. Hearing nothing in the room below, I turn to follow him. I'm used to living in cramped quarters, but these vents are stifling. I can feel the grease building up on my hands and knees as I maintain an uncomfortable crouch. My injuries pulse with each movement. The *deman* seems at home here.

We slither through the ductwork for a long time, taking a steadily rising path. Sometimes, we have to clamber up steeply slanted inclines. We're obviously moving toward the higher levels of the housing block. The moldy smell increases. I consider doubling back and breaking away, but even if I wanted to, the tunnels are too narrow to turn around with enough speed. He'd catch me before I got far, and much as I hate to admit it, I need him. He's the only one who can get me safely away from the commander's trap. After what he heard in my quarters, he has to believe I'm not working with her.

He maintains a punishing pace, hardly ever pausing to check direction. How long has he been here, within the palisade? The temperature continues to rise as we climb, the air becoming thicker as we move upward. Occasionally, he twists around to check on me, but he doesn't speak. I try to mirror his gait, but I'm much more clumsy. The fact that I'm wearing a robe over my pajamas doesn't help. I have to keep hitching it up to avoid tumbling. I could take it off, but these are the only clothes I have right now.

Finally, he stops and stretches an arm out to hold me back. He points at a metal grate in front of us. From what I can see, it looks pretty much the same as the one above my quarters, the one we were listening through. He bends forward to slide it aside. With a gesture for me to stay back, he pokes his head into the space below and looks around. It's dark, so whoever's quarters they are, the occupants are either not here, or they're asleep.

Apparently satisfied, he positions himself above the opening and jumps down feet first. I'm alone. I wonder if I should try to get away from him now. If I could find a way out of here, I might get back to the Temples' quarters and ask for their help, but how would I find my way out of this labyrinth without the *deman's* help? A beam of light flickers up from below. I back away as a thud sounds underneath me, and the light grows brighter.

"What are you doing?" The boy's voice startles me as he peers over the rim of the vent. I should have known I wouldn't be able to move quickly enough to escape. "Come over here and let me help you down."

I have no choice. He hoists himself into the duct and beckons to me. I pause, casting a longing glance down the tunnel we came from before sliding over to him. My ankle scrapes across the grate, and I wince. When I'm close enough, he wraps his arms around my waist. I try to jerk away, but he pulls me closer before flattening himself on his stomach beside the panel, still holding me tight, easing me into place over the opening. Beads of sweat break out on my forehead.

"Don't worry." His voice is calm. "Lower yourself down. There's a crate below. I'll hold you until your feet touch it." His arms are sure and strong, making me feel surprisingly steady as he nudges me over. I let myself dangle into the space below, allowing my body to drop until his arms are hooked under my shoulders. I clutch at his forearms and kick out with my feet, desperate for purchase.

"Easy. It's only a couple more inches. You're going to have to let yourself drop." His voice remains controlled despite the effort of holding me. He's unbelievably strong.

With no choice, I let myself fall. He hasn't lied. I land on something solid. I crouch down and run my fingertips over it. It's a wooden crate, its surface worn smooth. I swivel to take in the surroundings: a cramped rectangular room hardly bigger than a closet. The air is stale. There's a pallet covered in messy bedding crammed against the longer wall and a makeshift set of shelves holding what look like antique books made of real paper. A single lamp on the top of the bookcase illuminates the space.

"Stand back. I'm coming down." His voice echoes from the vent above.

I move from the crate to avoid getting crushed as he jumps. Then he's in front of me, large and looming.

"Where are we?" I ask.

"This is my room. We should be safe here." He steps off the crate and shoves it against the wall opposite the bed.

"Your room? How do you have a room here?"

"I guess I'll have to explain everything now. Would you like to sit, Daughter Wye?" He gestures to the crate.

"Please stop calling me that. My name is Omega."

"I hate those Greek letters. Can't I call you something else?" He folds his arms over his chest.

"Anything but Daughter Wye."

He strokes his furry jaw as he assesses me. "Hmm. How about Meg? You look like a Meg."

"Okay, I guess."

Waving me toward the crate, he plunks down on the bed, sitting cross-legged, like we used to in our elementary school classes.

"And what am I supposed to call you?" I ask, remaining on my feet.

"How about my name?"

"What's your name?" I cross my arms over my chest, mirroring his earlier stance.

A half-grin spreads over his face, one side of his mouth lifting higher than the other. "Since you asked so nicely, my name is Ghent."

"Ghent?" I try out the sound in my mouth. "That's a strange name."

"Sit down, would you? You're giving me a headache."

I perch on the edge of the crate. It's uncomfortable, but it's better than the floor. The *deman* breaks the silence. "You were telling the truth? About that commander? You're really not working with her?"

"Of course I'm not."

"Tell me what happened." His charcoal eyes are serious. He's wearing the same clothes as when we first met, dark shirt and trousers, wrinkled and dirty. His hair is tousled, dust streaks his face, but I can see how pale his skin is beneath all that dirt.

"The commander hurt you? Because of me?" He wipes his brow, leaving a trail of grime on his forehead.

"Who's Delta?" I ask.

He shoves a lock of his matted hair behind his ears. "My mother."

"You have a mother?"

"Of course. Don't you?"

"Yes, but you're a—"

"Person. Just like you."

I choke back a retort. He's not like me. Then I think back to what the Temples told me. I was born to a real monster myself, certainly more of a monster than this boy. He leans over and yanks off his socks, shoving them on top of a pile of rumpled clothes in the corner. This really is his room. A *deman's* room. Inside the palisade. Finally the pieces start to fall into place.

"Your mother," I say. "She's a Med-Tech?" That's why he was waiting for her outside the Clinic. That's how he knows first-aid. "What happened to her?"

"That's kind of a long story." He leans back on his elbows and stretches out, rolling his neck from side to side.

"Are we really safe here?" I ask.

"For now. This room is hidden behind a secret panel in my mother's quarters. It used to be a walk-in robe but Del – Delta – had it deleted from the plans so no one would know it was here. And the scanners don't operate in here either."

Not that there's anything to scan. Neither of us has a communicator.

"So who goes first?" I ask. Judging by his expression, he obviously has no idea what I'm talking about. I clarify, "Your story or mine?"

"I'll flip you for it." He pulls a copper disc out of his pocket and extends it to me.

"What's that?"

"A penny. Ancient currency. In the old days, this is how people made decisions." He plops the disc into my outstretched palm. It's dull and worn. I examine each side. On one, I can make out a face with a lot of fur around the jowls, more even than the boy standing in front of me. The other side of the disc is harder to make out. There are some words and vertical lines, but none of it makes any sense.

"What do I do with it?" I say.

"Throw it in the air and catch it. I'll call heads or tails and whatever comes up, that's who goes first."

"Tails?"

"Never mind." He takes the coin back, grazing my palm with his fingers. Just like when he took the knife from me outside the Clinic.

He tosses the token in the air and says "heads" before catching it and slapping it onto his wrist. "Tails. You first."

I feel as if I've been tricked, but there's nothing else to do for now so I tell him everything that happened to me since I met him. I speed up when I get to my encounter with the commander. I don't want to relive it in too much detail. He winces when I describe what she did to me, but doesn't interrupt. For some reason, I hesitate at the point when Upsilon returns me to my quarters. I'm not sure if I should tell him what the Temples told me, at least not yet. It's not important right now.

"Your turn," I say when I'm done with my own story minus the bit about my *deman* heritage. "What did your mother do that was so terrible? Other than hiding you, I mean."

"That's not enough?"

I realize how naïve I sound. "Why is it an issue now? You've obviously been here a while." I indicate the well lived-in state of his bedroom with its untidy piles of books and clothes.

He takes a deep breath. "Not her. Them."

"What do you mean?"

"I mean, I have two mothers."

I don't know why I didn't realize this was a possibility. It seems so unbelievable that not one, but two, women know about him. This boy has two mothers while I have only one.

"It's not that uncommon, you know." He sounds offended. "Lots of people have two mothers."

"Lots of *women* have two mothers." I can't help correcting him.

It's one of my faults actually, my desire to always be right about everything.

"You don't have two mothers," he says. His tone makes me sink back into the wall, but he ignores me and continues his story. His fingers flex around the edges of the mattress. He starts by telling me both his mothers' names: Delta, which of course I already know, and Epsie, short for Epsilon. Epsie is a history teacher, who gave up teaching to devote her life to Ghent, raising him, teaching him, and keeping him hidden.

Delta and Epsie were sweethearts from a young age. Epsie knew her Calling was motherhood even before she met Delta. Epsie wanted to become an Expectant soon after they got together, and she wanted Delta to be the one to administer the Procedure. Delta had only recently qualified as a Med-Tech, but she felt confident that she could do it. It would be a special bond between them. No one would know until after it was done.

They snuck into a Procedure Room in the middle of the night, so Delta could perform the implantation. The first trimester was uneventful. They avoided the Nest because it wasn't compulsory back then, and those who went there tended to wait until their second trimester. No one knew Epsie was an Expectant. She was a small woman anyway, and the only noticeable difference about her was that she had dark circles under her eyes from the morning sickness and lack of sleep.

Epsie began to show early in the second trimester, and the two women knew they would soon have to tell their friends. They wanted to do an ultra-scan to ensure all was well before telling anyone. They went to the Clinic late one night when no one was around, and Delta performed the unauthorized scan. She was good with the technology and able to delete the traces of her after-hours access to the system. But something went wrong. The way the *deman* tells it, Epsie had always felt something strange was happening before Delta even read the results of the scan. The scan only confirmed it. A male child. Conceived within the palisade.

Delta blamed herself. She realized they would have to terminate the fetus and delete all traces of what they did. She offered to perform the procedure that night but Epsie couldn't go through with it. She was so upset Delta had to sedate her. Delta didn't know what else to do. She told Ghent later that she had stayed up that whole night, worrying. The next morning Epsie had woken in good spirits. Delta was worried that Epsie had lost her mind during the night. She was talking about looking forward to impending motherhood. Delta knew she couldn't get psychological help for Epsie, not in her condition. No one could know Epsie was an Expectant. Epsie tried to explain that she had spent the night working out how to keep the child. Her idea was that Delta could monitor her condition and keep the medical records hidden. Epsie would wear loose clothing until her Expectancy became too obvious to hide. After that, she would simply stay out of sight for the duration, and Delta would cover for her saying she was ill or had gone on a retreat or something like that. As Ghent tells it, Epsie's next words to Delta that morning sealed the deal: "Think about it, Del. Fate has granted us this child. How can we ignore destiny?"

At that moment, Delta had known Epsie was right. Destiny or not, they had done this together, and they had to see it through. Whatever the consequences.

Chapter 12

I'm hanging on the boy's every word, wanting to know everything about his past. "Why did they call you Ghent?"

"What?" Ghent's shoulders sag. Telling me this much seems to have taken a toll on him. I realize with a start I'm probably the first person who's ever heard any of this.

"Why the name Ghent? Where did it come from?"

He shakes his head, causing his matted hair to flutter around his ears. "My mothers never liked the Greek letters."

"And I guess it would be weird for a boy"—I stumble over the unfamiliar word—"to be called Alpha or Beta or something."

"You don't think it's weird for *girls* to have those names?" He seems upset. I turn away, not knowing what I said wrong. There's a rustle of blankets and in a moment he's on his knees in front of me. The intensity of his gaze makes me feel weak. "Don't you see? It's another way the society controls you. Forces you to conform." He reaches for me, but I jerk away.

He massages his neck as if in pain. Then he looks over at the bookcase. "Hold on," he says as he rushes to it and traces his fingers along the cardboard edges that jut out along the shelves. Obviously searching for something. With a rush of breath, he pulls out an object. An antique book with a tattered cover. He flips it open. I can't hide my curiosity. I've never seen a paper book before. I move over to him and kneel by his side. He's not handling the object with the care I would expect. Instead, he flips through the pages with his thumb. The paper makes a crackling sound. I lean across until I can see the words, printed in real ink.

"Here it is. Listen to this." He looks up at me before turning his attention to the object in his lap.

He's going to read to me. A thrill of anticipation shoots through me. In a melodic voice, he begins, and it's as if a thousand butterflies have been released in my stomach.

"My father's family name being Pirrip, and my Christian name Philip, my infant tongue could make of both names nothing longer or more explicit than Pip. So I called myself Pip, and came to be called Pip. I gave Pirrip as my family's name, on the authority of his tombstone and my sister – Mrs. Joe Gargery, who married the blacksmith."

My eyes close as the ancient words fill me, rolling from the *deman's* tongue like silk. I've never heard anything this strange before, at least not from a book.

"Do you like it?" he asks.

My eyes fly open when I realize he's speaking to me.

"What is it?" I ask.

"It's called *Great Expectations*."

"I don't understand. What does it mean?"

"This part"—he taps his finger over the paragraph he read—"means that people didn't always use Greek letters for names. They were able to choose names for themselves. Even make up nicknames, like Pip did."

"That's not such a big deal. We use nicknames now. You call your mothers Del and Epsie," I say, but the words ring hollow. Nicknames don't seem like such a great innovation when we only have twenty-four names to choose from.

A small smile tugs at the corners of his lips. "And you said I could call you Meg." He reaches over and places the book on my lap.

I'm afraid to touch it. I've never held something so old or so precious.

"Here's what I read." He lifts my wrist and places my finger against the paper. The paper feels weird. It's rough and smooth at the same time. I examine the words with my fingertips, embarrassed at how cracked and dirty my nails are after crawling through the ducts.

"Why does his sister have such an odd name?" I ask.

"It's her husband's name," he explains.

"I don't understand."

"Joe Gargery. That's the name of her husband. In those days women used to take their husband's names."

Husband? I vaguely remember the term from history class. Something to do with the *deman* era. I have a sense it's a bad word, but it doesn't sound so scary on Ghent's lips.

I return to my original question, the one he never answered. "Is Ghent a nickname? Like Pip?"

"No, but my mothers did make it up for me."

"What does it mean?"

"It's the name of an old city, in a place that was once called Europe. No one knows if it even exists anymore. We lost contact with everything outside the walls so long ago. It was famous for education and trade."

"Really?" These are the things my mother talks about. Trade and new learning. According to the Temples, that's why she went outside the palisade. I shiver when I think about what happened to her, grateful for Ghent's warmth by my side.

I'm leaning so close to him that the book is almost crushed between us. He pries it away and returns it to the shelf. With his back to me, I notice the muscle beneath his shirt. When he turns to me, I'm struck by how human he looks. With a jolt, I realize we're the same. Neither of us should be here, but we both are because our mothers loved us more than they loved themselves. They were prepared to take big risks for us.

"What happened to Epsie? Where is your other mother now?" I pull my robe over my toes to warm my feet.

He hunches beside me, leaving enough room that we're not quite touching. "She's probably wherever Del is."

"And where is that?"

"I don't know." He rubs his hand across his jaw. "Epsie has a medical condition. It's serious. She's been getting worse for a while and we realized that eventually she'd have to be admitted to the Clinic. We also knew that as soon as they examined her, they'd discover she had been an undocumented Expectant. It was an impossible situation. I knew I'd have to run when she finally admitted herself to the Clinic. I'd have to get outside the palisade, get so far that no one could ever find me, so my mothers wouldn't get into trouble. If I was gone, they could make up some story about a miscarriage, and there'd be nothing to find when the authorities searched their quarters to check for evidence of living children."

"But you didn't want to leave?"

He turns aside, so I'm talking to his profile. I can't help but notice his high cheekbones and straight nose.

"No, but that wasn't the problem. Epsie wanted Del to take me away from here, so she could admit herself to the Clinic after the two of us were safely away. She'd heard tales of a sanctuary outside the boundary, where we might be safe. Even if the stories weren't true, I'd have a better chance outside the walls than within. Maybe I could even search for some of the lost cities"

Sanctuaries and lost cities, outside the palisade? Was my mother right all this time?

"Even if that's true, why would Delta agree to take you and leave Epsie behind?" I ask.

"She wasn't happy about it, but it was what Epsie wanted. Del has always done what Epsie wants."

"Why is Delta still here? Why didn't the two of you get away?"

"Epsie's condition deteriorated more quickly than we had expected. She collapsed a few nights ago and Del had to take her to the Clinic. There was no way around it. She knew Epsie would never forgive her for leaving me, so she told me to wait for her outside the Clinic. She'd come for me as soon as Epsie was stabilized. She never showed up."

"And you were waiting for her there when I found you?"

"Yes." He turns away and moves to the shelf where he picks up something, a flat object that had been lying beside the lamp.

"What's that?" I ask.

He offers it to me.

It's a piece of paper with an image emblazoned across it. All gray and white. Two women, beaming at each other. One is tall with short light hair, and the other is shorter with unruly dark hair, and dark eyes. I can see the resemblance to Ghent immediately in the smaller woman. The women are sitting on a sofa, holding hands.

"My mothers." Ghent is so quiet I can barely make out the words. "That's Delta." He points to the taller woman. "This is Epsie."

I examine the strange paper in awe. "What is this?"

"A photograph. Before we had digital tech, people used to take photographs with a substance called film. Epsie is an antiques collector." His voice breaks.

Returning the paper to him, I whisper, "I'm so sorry about your mothers."

He tenses. "I don't know where they are, but I have to know they're safe." He replaces the photograph on the shelf. "Anyway, it's not your problem, or your fault. Del was probably already in custody before you ever got to the Clinic that night." He wipes his face with his sleeve. "I've never told anyone any of this before. I've never spoken to anyone at all except my mothers."

The impact of his words strikes me like a physical blow. I crane my neck to look at him. "You've never been out of this room before your mothers disappeared?"

"Our quarters are bigger than this room. This is only my private space. I've been outside, too. A few times. Mostly at night when no one's around. I use the ventilation shafts."

That's how he knows his way around.

"You know you have to get outside the palisade, right? Whatever is going on with your mothers the commander knows you're around now. It's not safe for you to stay."

"I won't leave until I know my moms are safe." He paces

alongside the bed. He seems so large in the confined space. "And there's you to consider." He regards me in my dusty robe with my messed-up soggy hair. My cheeks flush. "They know that you've seen me. You're not safe either." I can almost see the idea brewing in his mind. "You have to come with me."

"Outside the palisade?" I ask.

He drops to his knees and clutches my wrists. "If we're both out of the way, the Protectors won't be able to do anything to them. There won't be any evidence of any wrongdoing."

"I can't." My mind reels with the risks and the possibilities. I want to see outside. I do. But this would be so permanent. If I left with him, there'd be no turning back. And what about my mother? What happens when she gets back and finds me gone?

"I can't," I repeat. "My mother wouldn't be safe. The commander's after her, too."

"That's a problem," he says. "We'd need some kind of insurance."

"What do you mean?"

"We'd need an airtight story," he continues. "One that even the commander would believe." He starts pacing again. "Something that would make her leave your mother alone. We'd need to do more than slip away. We'd need to leave proof that we've gone for good."

Gone for good. It's a scary thought. Exciting, but scary.

"What kind of proof?" I ask.

"I suppose we could leave a note," he says, "but they might not believe us. They might think I had kidnapped you and forced you to write it."

He can't be serious. He wants to stage a kidnapping? He finally stops pacing.

"Right, and the Protectors would form a search party and leave no stone unturned until they found us," I agree. "There's no way we'd escape them. Even with a head start."

Does the fact that I'm thinking this through mean I'd consider it? I shudder at the thought of Commander Theta and a band of Protectors hunting us through the wasteland. What if Delta and my mother are wrong? What if there's nothing out there? Ghent and I would die in the desert. Of starvation. Or worse.

"This is crazy. I can't leave." The realization crashes down on me. "I have to stay here, but I can make up a story. I'll say you kidnapped me and let me go. That way I could vouch for the fact you truly left and that you won't be a danger to anyone anymore." Ghent tries to interrupt but I keep going. "And I could get a message to your mothers. Let them know you made it out safely."

He drops onto his mattress. It takes him a few moments to form his next words and when he speaks, his voice is reedy. "I don't want to be alone."

My heart aches for him, but it's impossible. "I won't go with you. I can't."

None of this is his fault, but he has to get out of here, and it has to be alone. The strange thing is that the thought of leaving him makes me uncomfortable. Maybe it's guilt. If it weren't for me, he might have gotten away without the commander knowing for sure that he existed at all. I owe him.

"I'm sorry," he says on an exhale. "Of course you're right. I can't ask that of you. I'll go alone."

I hate the thought of what he'll have to go through out there, by himself.

"You don't have to be alone yet. We have to find out about your mothers."

He brushes off a blanket that has tangled around his foot, then rises from the bed.

"You must be hungry," he says, "and I'm sure you could use a painkiller if I can find one." Maybe this is an act to cover up his fear, but whatever it is, he's doing a convincing job. "Do you want to see the rest of our quarters?"

"Won't the Protectors be monitoring it?" I ask.

"Should be fine. As long as we come and go through the inside doors, they shouldn't detect us. The scanners are only triggered when the front door opens. This room opens directly to the inside of the quarters." He pushes against a concealed panel at the end of his bed, and it swings open to reveal a dark room beyond. "Wait here a second." He ducks out and returns a few moments later with what looks like an antique gas lamp. I've seen them before in the museum. "Can't risk the lights in case they're monitoring the power."

Guiding us with the lamp, he helps me through to the outer quarters. "Welcome to my world, Meg."

Chapter 13

The living area is large and well furnished, much like the Temples' quarters. There's a plush sofa with several matching arm chairs. I recognize it from the photograph of Ghent's mothers. There are two large picture windows. Passing me the lamp, Ghent moves into the darkness with easy grace. He rustles around, opening and shutting cupboards. A few moments later he returns with a box of supplies: nutri-bars, painkillers, and bottles of water. He places it on the coffee table and examines my feet. Despite being dirty and sore, my toes are sinking luxuriously into the carpet. I feel guilty at the thought of leaving marks and can't help remembering the mess I made of the Temples' carpet not so long ago.

"I think my mother's shoes might fit you," Ghent says, rubbing his chin. He ducks out of the room. While he's gone I lift the lamp to better illuminate my surroundings. The living area is even bigger than I thought. There's an impressive exercise station complete with treadmill and weights that are more high tech than the gym at my school. I had assumed Ghent's powerful build was attributable to what he is, that he has the brawn of the male of the species, but now I realize he works at it. There's probably not much else for him to do. I had always thought of my own life as pretty sheltered, but it's nothing compared to his. I try to hoist one of the weights but can hardly budge it. A tap against my elbow startles me. I wheel around to see his beaming face inches away.

"Try these." He takes the lamp from me and presses a pair of sturdy ankle boots into my hands, along with a clean pair of thick wool socks. The shoes look comfortable and well made, but I'm conscious they belong to one of his mothers. I slip on the socks first, and then the boots. Taking a few experimental steps, I almost overbalance. The shoes are too wide, but I should be able to walk if I'm more careful.

"Good?" he asks.

"Yes. Thanks."

He looks me up and down. "I should find you something else to wear."

I blush as I scan my ratty robe.

"But we should probably take this stuff back to my room first." He makes his way to the pile of supplies before pausing to ask, "While we're out here, do you need to...?" He points in the direction where I assume the bathroom is. I haven't had a chance to clean up since my shower earlier. The grime from the ducts covers my every pore and mats my hair. Clutching the lamp, I scurry in the indicated direction. Once inside the bathroom I lock the door.

Setting the lamp down, I examine the small space wondering why the bathroom is so tiny in such enormous quarters. I realize that it likely shares a wall with Ghent's room. His mothers probably remodeled it to give him more space. Everything in here is white: tiles, towels, fixtures. The lamplight bathes the room in shadows, making my reflection in the mirror seem alien. The hollows remain under my mismatched eyes. Strange that Ghent hasn't asked me about them.

Even in the dim light, I can see that my face is slicked with grease. My hair hangs in thick hanks around my shoulders. I gaze at the shower stall longingly, but I make do with splashing water on my cheeks and cleaning up as best I can. I try to pry some of the dirt from under my fingernails, but soon give up. There's a lavender soap. It smells heavenly, and I use it liberally on my hands, reveling in its soothing scent and soft, creamy texture for as long as I dare.

An antique comb sits on a shelf beside the mirror. I hope no one will mind if I use it. Wetting it first, I attack the worst of the tangles in my hair and gradually restore order to chaos. I reach into my pocket, relieved to find a hair tie. I use it to slip my hair into a ponytail before replacing the comb on the shelf. When I notice my reflection again, I'm surprised by the look of grim determination on my face. I'm going to get out of this mess somehow. And get Ghent outside the palisade.

When I leave the bathroom, the quarters are empty, and I panic for a few seconds before realizing that everything is exactly how we left it. Ghent must have gone back to his room. I head for the panel. It's slightly ajar. I tap before entering. Ghent's sitting cross-legged on the crate, wolfing down a nutri-bar.

"We need a plan," I say as I snap the panel back into place. My voice is surprisingly confident. "We need to find out about your mothers. You said Epsie was sick."

"It's a kidney problem," he says, offering me a nutri-bar. I wave it away even though I'm hungry. I need to focus. "She's had it most of her life, but Del has been able to keep it under control, until now."

"There must be a record of her in the Clinic, right?"

Ghent regards me with a scowl. "You don't think I thought of that already? I can't use any communications port without being discovered, and now neither can you."

That's true. With Commander Theta watching me, I can't access the communications system either, not even from a public terminal. "We'll have to ask someone else." I fold my arms over my chest and lean back against the wall, trying to project confidence I'm not sure I feel.

"Brilliant idea. Why didn't I think of that?" He shoves the last morsel of the nutri-bar into his mouth.

"Don't get mad at me. We're in this together now."

Ghent is on his feet, pacing again. Tension crackles in the air around us.

"Who can we ask for help?" he says.

I shake my head, then look up at his eyes. They remind me of someone else, another set of warm brown eyes, soft and reassuring. "Gamma Temple. Her mother is a Med-Tech."

Ghent's brows shoot up as he strides forward and grabs my elbows, gripping them too tight. I cringe as pain shoots through my arm. "Did you say *Temple?* We can't talk to them. Please tell me you didn't say anything to the Temple family about me."

"Ghent, what's wrong?"

"The Temples! They're all that's left of an old religious order. They believe that men are evil, should be tortured, and killed. They were amongst those who planned the palisade and drove the men away in the first place. What did you tell them?"

He releases my arms and rakes his fingers through his hair, causing it to stick out in messy spikes. I clasp my hands together to steady them. "Ghent, they're my friends. They know nothing about you. I promise."

He paces across the room and leans into the wall, pressing his head into his forearms. Sweat stains his collar, and his hair is still a mess.

"Ghent, please."

Finally, he looks in my eyes as if he can read the truth there. He lifts a hand to my face, stopping short of making contact. I think he's trying to say that he trusts me. Not quite sure how to broach the subject again, I take a deep breath before speaking. "Hear me out. You don't have to agree, and I won't mention it again, but please listen at least once."

He squints as if he's in pain.

"Gamma Temple's a friend," I start.

He moves past me and slumps on the crate. I join him, maintaining a little distance, at least as much as possible on the small box.

"I know it's a long shot," I say, "but she may be able to help find out something about your mothers. Her mother is a Med-Tech, and Gamma may be able to access her datapad."

"It's too dangerous." Ghent's face is ashen. The Temples scare him. But he can't be right about them. Ma Temple helped my mother hide the truth about me and my ... *father*. For all this time.

Maybe if I tell him that part of my story, he'll believe me, he'll let them help us.

"There's something I haven't told you, about what the Temples did for me," I say. "I think it will make you understand, that you can trust them. They kept a secret for me and my mother. An important secret. They protected us."

"What kind of secret?"

It's surprisingly hard to say it out loud. It's going to be the first time I've ever admitted it to anyone. "I'm not a true daughter of the palisade," I say. "I come from somewhere else." I stumble to find the right words.

"I don't understand. I looked you up in the data stream. Your mother is Sigma Wye. You were born in the Nest."

"Yes, that's true, but this isn't where I was made. My mother never had the Procedure."

Ghent's eyes widen but he doesn't interrupt.

"My mother was curious about what's outside the walls."

Ghent places a hand on my forearm. Somehow it steadies me. When I don't continue he asks, "She went outside?"

I dip my head.

"So, you were created the natural way, the way men and women…" his voice trails off.

"Yes. In some ways, I have less right to be here than you."

"You have every right to be here." He lets go of my arm and grabs my shoulders, turning me to face him. "So your mother knows what's outside the palisade? Can we ask her?"

"No, she's at a retreat. You can't afford to wait. I don't know how long it will be before she comes back. Anyway, even if she knows anything, it probably won't help. If she knew anything helpful, she would have reported it to the Elders long ago. We'd all know about it by now."

Ghent digs his nails into the crate. "Okay, but I don't understand what any of this has to do with the Temples."

"They helped my mother hide the truth, falsified the data

stream, gave her contact lenses to hide my eyes."

"So that explains it."

He *had* noticed them before.

"But what about your true father?" he asks. "Where is he? Who is he?"

My eyes sting as I think about what happened to my mother outside the palisade all those years ago. Helpless and alone.

"I see," Ghent says. He pats me awkwardly on my good knee before pulling away. "I'm so sorry. I can see now why you were so scared of me."

"No, that's not it. When I met you, I didn't even know about him. I only found out after the Commander got to me."

Ghent drops his head and speaks so softly it's hard to make out his words. "I understand, Meg. I truly do. And I'm so, so sorry for what happened to you. But the fact that the Temples helped you, helped your mother, that doesn't necessarily prove that I can trust them."

I want to contradict him, but I know what he means. Helping women is one thing. Ma Temple was protecting my mother from what she saw as the monsters outside. That doesn't mean she'd help protect a boy inside the walls, even if he hadn't done anything wrong. I decide to approach the problem from another angle.

"Gamma and I have been friends forever," I say. "We don't have to involve her mother. Gamma can hack the datapad herself. She's done it before. And even if you're right about the Temples, remember I'm in this too now. I don't want the Protectors to get to me any more than you do. We're in this together."

He leans forward and cradles his face in his hands. Then he presses his fingers against the bridge of his nose. "You know where I live. I can't risk it. I can't let you leave here without me. If they get to you, even if you don't mean to tell them anything, they might get it out of you."

I know he's right, but the situation is impossible.

"You can't come with me to see Gamma," I say.

Ghent runs trembling fingers through his hair. Suddenly, he darts across to the bed, reaching for something under the mattress. I leap to my feet and watch him fossick until he pulls out a small device. He brushes it off with the hem of his shirt. It's made of metal, not much bigger than the penny he showed me earlier, but thicker and slightly rounded on one side.

"What is that?" I ask.

"Transmitter. My mothers sometimes use it to get messages to me."

Warnings, I realize, if someone is coming to their quarters. My heart cracks at the thought of how he's had to live his whole life.

"Why didn't Delta take it with her to the Clinic?" I ask.

"I don't know." Ghent flips the object over in his palm. "I guess she didn't think of it when Epsie collapsed. She was too worried about her or she may have been worried someone would see it and ask questions." He reaches under the mattress and pulls out a second object, similar in size and shape. He holds both of them out to me.

"This one's the transmitter," he explains, extending the one in his left hand. "The other is the receiver. It's one way. You could talk to your friend. And I'd get the message through this. We wouldn't have to stay together. But it has limited range. I'd still have to come with you part of the way." Ghent is carefully examining the equipment, causing little bursts of static to punctuate his words.

"How close do you need to be for me to transmit?" I ask. "Perhaps I could sneak it into the Temples' quarters from here? We must be nearby, right?"

"We're on the same floor as the Temples, only a few doors down. But we can't risk it. There's too many Med-Techs around and we know at least some of them are working with the Protectors." I cringe as I think about Rho Zee. Most of the Med-Techs live on this floor. I hunker down on the crate, feeling suddenly exposed even though I know we're relatively safe here. "And if you're wrong about your friend. If she sounds the alarm…" Ghent doesn't have to finish the sentence. There's at least one Protector stationed in this very building, in my quarters, and she has a hotline to Commander Theta.

"I'll have to catch Gamma when she's not at home. Somewhere there won't be Med-Techs or Protectors." Suddenly it hits me. "The factory. I might be able to catch Gamma alone there, without anyone seeing me. She usually sneaks up to the storage room at some point during the day. And I know a back way in."

"Will the transmitter work from, say, a hundred feet away?" I estimate the distance from the storage room to the hiding spot I have in mind.

"Probably." Ghent rolls the device around in his palm. "What are you thinking?"

"There's a loading bay out back with a shed that's hardly ever used. You could hide there. It's never locked so it shouldn't be difficult for us to get in."

"You're sure about this?"

"Yes." I wish I could sound more confident, but this is the only plan I have.

"Alright then." Ghent's tone is all business now. "When's Gamma's next shift?"

"She should be back on the line tomorrow morning." Daylight. That could be tricky. It'll be harder to keep Ghent out of sight. "If you're going to be hiding in the shed by the time her shift starts, we'll have to plant you there tonight. What time is it?"

Ghent lifts an object from the top of the bookcase. An antique timepiece. It's very elegant, with a worn leather band housing a gold circle covered with a shiny layer of glass. I've seen pictures of them before. They only tell the time and nothing else. They can't be used to track people.

"It's almost midnight," Ghent says. "You must be exhausted."

I've been running on adrenaline for so long I haven't noticed how tired I am until he mentions it. I stifle a yawn.

"Why don't you get some sleep? We have time" He indicates his mattress. "I'll keep watch. We'll be able to make it to the factory before dawn."

Despite my exhaustion, I'm uncomfortable taking his bed. I'm not sure if I can sleep with him hovering nearby.

"Maybe we should take turns getting some rest?" I suggest. "You sleep first, and I'll keep watch."

He laughs out loud. I suppose he's not too convinced about the idea of me guarding him. My cheeks flush.

"Oh, alright." I give in. "You're sure it'll be safe?"

"I'll be right here." He pats the bedcovers. I sigh and move toward him as he straightens the sheets. When he moves, I slip my feet out of his mother's shoes and climb under the covers. The bed is warm and soft, and the blankets smell of Ghent, oak and lavender. The soap from the bathroom I now realize. I nestle my head into the pillows as he scoops up an extra blanket from the foot of the bed and drapes it over me. The last thing he says before taking up his vigil is, "Sleep well, Meg."

Surprisingly, I do.

Chapter 14

"Wake up! Are you alright?"

I force my eyes open. Ghent is leaning over me, shaking my shoulders. I bolt up, dizzy and disoriented, before remembering where I am. In his quarters. On his bed. "What happened?"

"You were crying out. I tried to wake you, and you pushed me away." I scrub at my cheeks and realize they're wet. A nightmare. I wonder how loud I was screaming. I sniffle as he fetches a bottle of water and a nutri-bar from his supply pack. He passes them over and sits beside me. The lavender scent is stronger now. He must have cleaned up while I slept. His hair is damp and slicked back, and he's wearing different clothes, loose dark trousers and a black short-sleeved shirt. The dark color emphasizes the paleness of his skin.

I bite into the nutri-bar gratefully even though it's soggy and a little stale. "What time is it?" I manage around a mouthful.

"Almost five thirty."

I snap to attention. "We have to go, and you haven't slept."

"You needed it more." He says, looking away. He clears his throat. "We're going to have to get moving soon. Are you up to it?"

He let me sleep later than he should have. The sun rises early in summer and we'll have to be in place outside the factory before the morning shift. I feel bad that he hasn't had any rest. At least he had a chance to clean up. If he makes it outside the palisade, he may never see soap again. He may die in the wasteland. My nightmare floods back to me – Ghent's body decomposing in the desert, buzzards picking at strips of his rotting flesh.

"What are you thinking?" He hesitates before touching my shoulder. I glance over at him willing my dream out of my mind. His solid frame fills so much of the tiny space. I can't bear to think of it reduced to a mound of sun-bleached bones.

"Nothing."

* * *

Making it to the factory before dawn turns out to be pretty easy. We're traveling light: only the clothes we're wearing and Ghent's pack of supplies. My hair is swept back in a tight braid to keep it out of the way. Using the ducts to get out of the housing block isn't so hard, partly because it's a downhill climb and partly because I'm less claustrophobic this time. It's also easier to maneuver in the clothes Ghent gave me from his mothers' closet, a simple dark shift over durable cotton trousers. My injuries bother me less today. Although my arm stings a little, the swelling on my knee has gone down almost to nothing.

Ghent sets a punishing pace, but somehow I manage to keep up. We make good time to the shed. We'll have to wait here for the night crew to clock off before I can take up my position inside the factory. Luck is on our side. The shed is not only unlocked, but its back corner houses some warped shelving where Ghent can conceal himself. There's even an old tarpaulin he can hide under. We attempt a few trial runs with the transmitter. Each time, I move a little farther away to check the range. I try a final run up the factory's outside staircase, all the way to the emergency exit. The transmitter relays my test message without a hitch.

When I'm safely back in the shed, the buzzer sounds, followed by movement at the front of the factory. The night crew is heading home. In a few moments, the day shift will arrive. I have to get to the upper walkway before there are enough people to notice me sneaking in. I can hide in the supply room and wait for Gamma to put in an appearance. Ghent gives me the signal to get moving, but before I do, he reaches out to stop me. He tugs at the collar of my shirt, double-checking the placement of the transmitter.

His voice is uneven. “Be careful.” He reaches for a stray strand of my hair and tucks it behind my ear. Only yesterday I would have thought he was trying to hurt me with those powerful hands. Now I see a real person: pale skin, dark hair and dark eyes, tall with a muscular frame, and a lightly asymmetrical face, one lip quirking a little higher than the other when he smiles, a brow that furrows into a curious “v” when he’s trying to work something out. He’s a person like me. In many ways, he’s less of an anomaly than I am. At least his mothers planned for him to be here.

“Meg.” He nudges me to get my attention. “Promise you’ll be careful.”

“I will. If I get into any trouble, I’ll give you the signal.” I hope it doesn’t come to that.

We stand face to face in the tiny shed. He towers over me, feet planted wide, arms at his sides. His lips purse and unpurse as if he wants to say something. But I don’t give him the chance. I turn for the door. The first beams of the morning sun illuminate my way as I climb up the outside staircase to the emergency exit. I try to turn the handle, realizing belatedly that I should have tested it before. I should have known my luck wouldn’t hold. Of course, it’s locked. I hadn’t foreseen that. I’ve only ever opened it from the inside. I throw my shoulder against it, but it doesn’t budge. How could I have been so stupid?

“Ghent!” I hiss into the transmitter. “The door’s locked!” I charge for the stairs. Maybe we can both hide in the shed and formulate another plan. When I’m halfway down, I barrel into a figure bolting up. Ghent. He’s holding something. A small metal clip. He grabs my upper arms to steady us both.

“I can fix it,” he says.

“We don’t have time.” I try to shove him away, back down the stairs, but he pushes past me, almost sending me over the railing, and starts fidgeting with his new device at the lock.

I race up beside him. “What is that?”

"My version of a skeleton key. I can override the lock with it."

I wonder how many other tricks he's picked up with only his books and his mothers for company. The thought is unsettling. I'm no slouch with technology. But this *deman* is something else. It's strange to think that despite being locked away his whole life, he has more useful skills than I learned in all my cycles at school.

The volume of workers' voices increases.

"Ghent!" I grab at his arm to pull him away as the door swings open. He flashes me a triumphant smile.

"Get out of here." I turn him toward the stairs.

Without a word, he complies. I wait until he's safely back in hiding. Then I slip into the factory, hurrying across the upstairs walkway to the storage area. The lights are dim. They haven't yet gone to full strength for the day shift. Without my communicator, I can't unlock the storage room door automatically, but this one is easy enough to crack. Gamma taught me how to do it when we both started working here. After a little recoding, the door opens.

The room is dark, so I feel my way to a low shelf where I can hide behind several of the larger dye barrels. It won't be safe to move around until the day shift starts up. The air is thick and stale. They don't go through much dye during the night. I'm probably the first person in here since yesterday. It's also cold. It takes a while for the sun to heat things up. I rub my hands together and blow on them.

"Ghent," I whisper into the transmitter at my collar. "I'm in. I hope you're hearing me. The shift will start in a moment."

The machines should be warming up soon. My legs cramp. It seems like an eternity before the second buzzer sounds and the whooshing and pumping of the machinery crescendos. The chatter of the girls rises in volume in concert with it. They have to talk loud to be heard over the din. I figure it's safe to whisper an update: "Ghent. The shift has started. Sit tight."

It's warmer now. I imagine Ghent pressed into the corner of

the shed, hiding under the stinky tarpaulin. He's probably as cramped and uncomfortable as I am. Eventually, I decide it's safe to push myself out of my hiding place. I groan as I straighten my legs. No sooner do my muscles relax than the storage room door opens. Raised voices approach. Startled, I dive back into my hiding spot, calf muscles screaming in protest.

"Why didn't you want to come up?" It's a young woman's voice, vaguely familiar.

"It's a bit early for this, isn't it?" says another girl.

Gamma. She must be with Chi again. My heart pounds against my ribs.

"That's never bothered you before." Chi's voice is syrupy sweet. They're coming closer to where I'm hiding. I crawl back into the shelf. "What's with you today?"

"Nothing." Gamma sounds exasperated.

"Hey, if you don't want to be with me, say so. It's not like I don't have other options."

"Fine." Gamma's voice is quiet.

"Then, c'mon." Chi's voice has returned to that silky tone.

"No. I mean fine. Find someone else," Gamma says.

"You don't think I will?"

"I don't care."

"I could easily have someone else by tomorrow, and you'd be alone."

"How do you know *I* haven't found someone else?" Gamma says.

If she has, that was fast work. She was with me last night in her quarters and ... *oh*.

Chi's laugh is derisive. "Have a nice life, Gamma."

I hear the door open and close. Chi must have left, but I don't know where Gamma is. I can make out her breathing nearby, but I can't get a sense of direction. She huffs, and there's a loud clank. She must have kicked one of the dye barrels. She's not in the mood I was hoping for, but she's here. This is my chance to talk to her alone. I sneak out from my hiding place, slowly unfurling my limbs. Following the sound of her breathing, I realize she must be closer than I thought. Sounds like she's in the next aisle over. I carefully make my way towards the sound of her breaths.

"Gamma," I say.

She whirls around. It's hard to make out her features in the dim light. "Omega?"

"Are you alright? I didn't see you on the line." She moves forward and her words come out in a rush. "I suppose you heard all that."

"I'm sorry."

"Don't be." I wish I could see her better, but I don't want to turn on the lights.

"Why didn't I see you downstairs?" she asks suspiciously. "Did you clock in with us?" She takes a step closer. "And what are you wearing?"

"Oh this? They're old. Mom's."

"You're not keeping up with the laundry either, are you?" She leans against a shelf. "I'm sorry about last night. I guess all of that was a bit of a shock. Are you really okay now?"

"Can we talk about something else?"

"Do you have a topic in mind?"

"Actually, I do," I say, crossing my fingers at my side.

"Oooh, I'm intrigued. Do tell."

I try to keep my voice light and gossipy. "I'm curious about something I heard in the Clinic the other night. I didn't get a chance to ask you about it yesterday. I wondered if you or your mom might know anything about it." I hope Ghent won't freak out that I mentioned Ma Temple. I rehearsed this about a hundred times last night without saying her name, but it slipped out anyway. "It's probably not even true, but some women were talking about a Med-Tech, a Delta Jaye?"

Gamma scrunches her brow. "You heard about that? I wonder how it got out? I've heard some wild rumors about that woman.

You're probably right that they're not even true. I mean, if they were true there'd be Protectors everywhere. There would have to be if we actually had *demen* loose inside the palisade."

With her fingers resting against my forearm – when did that happen? – she must sense my shiver.

"What's wrong?" she asks.

"I'm sorry," I splutter, trying to recover my composure. "It's my arm. From the factory. I guess it's still a little sore."

"I didn't even think to ask about it with everything else going on. You probably should be home resting. Do you want me to take you?"

"I'm fine." I try to make my voice sound casual. "But I'm interested in what you were saying."

"Maybe we should go outside and get you some air?" she says.

I'm prepared to take the risk of talking to her outside. It won't do any harm as long as we go out the back stairs and no one sees us. She doesn't seem to think I'm involved with the *deman*. I don't protest when she loops an arm through mine to lead me to the door.

"I don't want anyone to see me here," I say, remembering that I didn't actually clock in, and I'm still not wearing my contacts.

"Oh, so you *are* playing hooky?" She opens the door. "Don't worry. You know how good I am at sneaking around." She guides me to the emergency exit by the back stairwell, unwittingly retracing my earlier steps. Pushing the door open she ushers me down the stairs. I don't think anyone could hear us over the din of the machinery, and I'm pretty sure we've managed to keep out of sight.

"This way." She grabs my wrist and makes for a small patch of grass dotted with shrubs about fifty feet behind the shed. My heart thumps as we pass, knowing Ghent is so close. Gamma helps me to the ground behind the bushes, out of sight of anyone who might come outside for a cigarette. She kneels beside me, and notices my eyes in the daylight. "Omega, why didn't you put your contact lenses in?"

"I lost them."

"Don't you have a spare set?"

"I couldn't find them either."

"No wonder you've gone into hiding. Do you want me to call Mom? She could probably arrange a new set."

"No. I mean, not just yet. I really want to know about Delta."

"Okay, but after that you have to go home, alright? I'll call Mom about your lenses."

In the sunlight, I notice the light spray of freckles across her nose, and I wonder if they control for that in the Procedure. I've never thought to ask, but I always felt they suited Gamma. Did her mother design them, like they design everything else about us?

"Earth to Omega." Gamma waves a hand in front of me. "Tell me the rumor you heard, and I'll see how closely it matches what I heard."

Something bangs in the shed. Ghent, warning me not to trust Gamma.

"What was that?" Gamma says, looking right at the shed.

"It's nothing. Probably an animal." I tug at her forearm to get her attention. "At the Clinic yesterday some women said something about a *deman* inside the palisade, and the name – Delta. I didn't hear any more. But it's really strange, right?" I try to keep my tone light. I hope she doesn't think there's any more to this than good old-fashioned curiosity.

Finally, she takes the bait. She clutches my knee as she speaks. "I overheard Mom on her communicator. There's a rumor that this Delta and her partner have been harboring a *deman* forever. Can you believe it? And he *escaped*. He's supposed to be loose inside the palisade somewhere. And it gets even weirder. They're also saying the *deman* is their *son*."

"Does your mother know what happened to Delta?" I hope

I'm not pushing too hard. I don't want to rouse her suspicions any further, but she's our best lead.

"I'm not sure. I didn't hear the whole conversation, but it sounded like her partner was ill, and they're keeping them together."

"In the Clinic?"

"I don't know. Why?" Gamma leans back on her heels. I'm digging too deep. I know it. Another thump sounds from the shed.

"I wonder what kind of animal that is," Gamma says as she scrambles to her feet and motions for me to follow. "Let's go find out."

"No." My voice is too loud as I reach out to pull her back down. She raises an eyebrow and I try to come up with a believable explanation for my actions. "I don't want anyone to see me out here."

"Don't worry. I'll go take a quick look. Be right back." She pats my arm as she slips away.

I peer around the hedge to see that she's heading straight for the shed. It's quiet except for the distant sounds of birdsong and the odd coyote howling in the distance. Even the machine noise from the factory seems strangely muted. Ghent's trapped. He can't get out of the shed unnoticed, and even if he could, there's nowhere to go. I speak low into the transmitter, "Ghent, don't move. She won't look in there if you don't make a sound." I hope I'm right. "Ghent, please. I hope you can hear me."

Gamma wanders around searching for the source of the noise. She hasn't gone near the shed door. She's still investigating around the side panel, but she's getting awfully close. I hope Ghent heard me. I hope he takes my advice. "Ghent. I've got this under control. Please stay there." I realize that if he can hear my transmission, Gamma might be close enough to hear it too. I bite down on my lip. *Stupid, stupid, stupid.*

I don't know if Gamma heard me though the communicator or

through the bushes, but she calls out. "Did you say something?"

I crawl out and point toward the nearest pasture. "I saw something. It went that way."

She spins to look in the direction I'm indicating, a fallow field, covered in a small layer of weeds.

"What did it look like?" she asks.

"I don't know. Small. Like a groundhog."

"Pretty noisy groundhog."

"Maybe it was a raccoon."

"In the daylight?"

"Gamma, please come back."

She takes a last look around, shrugs her shoulders and scampers back to where I'm hiding.

"Do you want to go home now? I could call Mom about those contacts. Or I could even say I'm sick and go back with you. We could play hooky together. Just like when we were at school."

A day cavorting around with Gamma, and Ghent listening in, is not exactly part of the plan. Unless…

"Can we go to the Clinic?" I ask.

Her nose wrinkles. "Why would you want to go there?"

"I was thinking. About Delta. That rumor."

"Like we could maybe check it out?" She claps her hands together like a child. Her honeysuckle fragrance wafts around me, and I feel guilty for using her like this.

"Do you think we could?"

"I don't see why not. If I call in sick, they'll make me check in with Mom anyway, and she's doing rounds at the Clinic today." She presses her fingers to her lips. "But I'd have to figure out how to explain you."

"I'd wait outside." I sit up straighter as the idea begins to take shape.

"No way. This is our adventure. We'll do it together." Her expression brightens. "I'll go to Mom's office to check in with her, and let you into the Clinic by the back way."

"What if someone sees?" I ask.

"We'll disguise you. There must be some way to hide those eyes. We'll just have to keep out of sight until I think of something. I have to report to Tau so I can clock out," she says. "Will you be alright here?"

As I watch her head back to the factory I wonder if this is the right thing to do. I lower my lips to the transmitter so they're almost brushing against the metal. "Ghent. Stay where you are. Gamma's going to take me to the Clinic to find your mothers. Can you follow at a safe distance?"

Silence.

"Ghent. Can you hear me?"

I'm answered by a scraping sound. Metal against dirt. I peer around the bushes to see what's happening. The shed door clangs shut as Ghent charges toward me, low to the ground, covered with his cloak. He had twisted it through the straps of his pack earlier but he must have taken it out for the extra cover. He falls beside me, panting. "Meg, don't do this. It's too dangerous. I'll go to the Clinic. Tonight. By myself." His words are clipped as he gasps for breath. I'm horror-struck. He can't be here. Gamma will be back any second.

I grasp his wrist, my fingers barely encircling it, and speak in a wobbly voice. "Get back to the shed."

He pulls his arm away and kneels in front of me. "Only if you promise you won't go through with this. Make up an excuse to get away from her."

"No! This is our best chance." Then it dawns on me. He's worried about me. He's risking himself out here in the daylight to protect *me*.

When he speaks again his voice is sharp. "Don't you understand? She's a *Temple*. This is a trap."

He may be right, but we don't have any choice. He can't go waltzing into the Clinic after dark. He needs to be outside the palisade by then.

"We can trust her." My fingers rake against the dry ground, causing dirt to grind underneath my nails.

"Omega?" It's Gamma's voice.

We're trapped. I can't see her yet, but there's no way Ghent will make it back to the shed before she gets to us. He grips my shoulders and shoves me further into the bushes, urging me to move away from Gamma. Then he scrambles to his feet, maintaining his crouch and tries to pull me along with him. I shake him off. Shoving him into the bushes, I raise a finger to my lips. He knows what I'm going to do and I can tell from his expression that he doesn't like it. He reaches up to cover my mouth, but before he can catch me, I call out to Gamma.

"Coming!" I force my voice to sound cheery as Ghent sinks back to the dirt. I start to move in Gamma's direction. She'll be able to see me in a moment. Ghent reaches out to stop me, but with one more step, I'm in Gamma's sightline.

"There you are." She calls out from a distance that's way too close for comfort. "I'm officially off shift. Let's get out of here."

Chapter 15

Gamma drags me around the side of the Clinic where we clamber over an uneven stone patio, weeds poking through the cracks, adjacent to the back door. From here, the building doesn't seem so imposing. Unlike the front entrance with its glass doors and cobblestone pathway, the back section comprises only a few yards of craggy boulders set around a derelict garden before hitting the fence-line.

"I'm going around front," Gamma says. "I'll come get you in about fifteen minutes. No one should see you here, but if anyone comes, hide behind those rocks." She squeezes my hands between hers. "This isn't the first time I've done this." She taps a thoughtful finger to her lips, looking me up and down. "Once we get inside, we're going to have to find some way to hide those eyes, though."

"You think?" I'm getting a bad feeling about this.

"Trust me." She tugs on my three middle fingers, in that familiar gesture from our childhood. Her skin is smooth, her hands tiny and delicate compared to Ghent's large rough ones. There's been no sign of him since we left the factory, but even if the transmitter isn't working, he knows where we're heading so hopefully he's not too far away.

"We good?" Gamma smiles before ducking around the corner. As soon as she's out of sight, I press against the outside wall, trying hard to be invisible.

"Ghent?" I whisper into the transmitter. "I don't know if you can hear me, but I'm at the back of the Clinic. I'm going to find your mothers."

The only response is the scuttling of some creature through the grass. I hope it's not a snake. I have no idea how much time has passed since Gamma went inside. There's a shuffling noise behind the rocks, and my every muscle tenses. Before I have time to go into full panic mode, the door swings open and Gamma steps out. She grabs me by the wrist and pulls me inside, dropping into a mock curtsey. "Voila!"

As the door closes, I chance a glimpse at the rocks, unsure whether I only imagine a shadow out there. Gamma and I are alone in a narrow corridor. The linoleum is warped and several light bulbs are blown. The air smells faintly of disinfectant.

"This way." She directs me toward a storage closet and shoves me in.

"What are you doing?" I ask, whipping my head around to gauge the surroundings.

Gamma snaps on an overhead light and indicates a shelf behind her. There are a couple of old cleaners' uniforms: dark gray coveralls coated with a thin film of dust. "The disguise you ordered, ma'am."

"What?"

"It's perfect. As a cleaner, you can go anywhere. No one will notice you." I'm about to object, but she ignores me. "I found out what room those women are in. Managed to check the directory in my mother's office. It's in intensive care and there's a guard, but as a cleaner you can slip right past."

"What about my eyes?"

Gamma brandishes a cap, then plunks it on to my head with a flourish. She has to lift up on tiptoes to pull the visor down. "That should do it," she says, "if you keep your head down."

I flick the cap off and scrunch it in my fist. "You're crazy."

"That's what makes me so much fun." She winks and flashes me a grin.

"Gamma, do you think I can do this?"

"What's the worst that can happen?" She reaches for the coveralls, patting off the dust before helping me slip them over my clothes. This involves hitching up the shift I borrowed from Ghent's quarters. The cleaner's uniform was made for someone shorter so my borrowed trousers peek out below the cuffs. I fasten the top buttons myself and adjust the collar so Gamma won't see the transmitter hidden inside. There are no boots in the closet so I have to leave on the shoes I'm wearing. Ghent's mother's shoes. Hopefully, they'll pass muster if anyone bothers to look at my feet. Gamma puts together a makeshift bucket of cleaning supplies from another shelf. As a final touch, she twists my braid into a knot, piles it on my head and slaps the cap back on top of it, adjusting the visor over my eyes.

"You know the way to intensive care?" she asks. "I can only take you part way. I'll have to get back to Mom's office before she misses me. When you're done in the ICU, you'll have to make your own way out. Head out the front door in the uniform during the shift change. No one will notice you as long as you keep your head down. Come by my place later and tell me what happened."

That'll be a good place to hide out. Until Theta's guard is out of my quarters, I have no place else to go. Gamma takes me as far as she can, before pointing me toward intensive care. "Room two-one-three. It'll be the one with the guard at the door."

"Do you really think I can fool a guard?" I say.

"You can do it. Just sneak in, sneak out and … come over after?"

The next move is mine. If I'm going to do this I have to move. Now. Without warning, Gamma leans across and pecks me on the cheek. "Go for it."

With that, she's gone.

I let my feet take me in the right direction. The walls are bright white and the lights are harsh in this corridor. Printed signs indicate the different wards. It's the middle of the shift, so the hallways are relatively quiet. Med-Techs and Aides are making their rounds but without the hustle and bustle that accompanies shift changes. The scent of antiseptic and bleach is stronger here. The few staff I pass don't seem to notice me. I force myself on, my footfalls muffled against the linoleum. The door at the top of the stairwell is closed. I grasp the knob, but don't turn it. Once I do, there'll be no turning back.

Taking a breath for luck, I open the door to peer into the corridor. Ghent's mothers' room is immediately obvious. A Protector slouches outside, red hair clashing with the black uniform. She seems bored, staring at her communicator. I walk forward with all the confidence I can manage. Stopping in front of her, careful to keep my head down, I mumble, "Cleaning service, room two-one-three."

"Weren't you here a couple of hours ago?" she asks.

"Uh, not me, ma'am." I lower my voice in an attempt to disguise it. "Would you like me to check with my boss?"

The Protector lifts her communicator to make a call. She's not going to give me any choice. I'll have to run. My muscles tense. I doubt I can outrun her but I'll have to try. A loud bang comes from the stairwell. The Protector pushes me aside. The stairwell door opens and a set of fingers curls around its edge, large *deman* fingers, followed by a shock of messy dark hair right before the door slams shut again.

Ghent.

He's creating a diversion, so I can get into his mothers' room.

"Wait here." The Protector presses me against the wall and heads for the stairs.

This is it.

The second she's out of sight, I open the door. The room is sparse. Both women are here, both of Ghent's mothers, each a little older than in the image he showed me. Epsie lies unmoving on the bed, attached to several beeping machines, her tousled dark hair, so like Ghent's, splayed out over the crisp white pillow. Her eyes are closed, a plastic tube taped across her nose and mouth. Delta is sitting in an orange chair beside the bed, holding her hand. She's tall with short blonde hair and tired ice-blue eyes. Her grip tightens around her partner's hand as she stares at me.

"Something going on?" Her voice is deep, controlled. A

muscle in her jaw twitches, reminding me of Ghent.

As I move forward, she stands, effectively blocking Epsie from me.

"Don't worry. I'm with Ghent." My words come out in a rush. The color drains from her face. "I'm helping him."

She looks me up and down. Her breath hitches when her gaze lands on my shoes. "Where did you get those?"

"He gave them to me."

Her knuckles turn white around Epsie's hand.

"I can't stay long," I say. "Your son distracted the guard, but she'll be back. He needs to know you're alright. Both of you. He won't go outside the palisade until he knows you're safe."

Before Delta can respond, there's a commotion in the hall. The guard is returning. I need more time. Grabbing one of the cleaning rags from my bucket, I race to the windowsill, pretending to dust it.

"Everything okay in here?" The Protector's voice is gruff as she strides into the room. Delta sinks back into the plastic chair.

"You." The Protector points to me. "Are you hearing impaired? I told you to wait outside."

"I thought I should get started," I say in my fake cleaner's voice. "Didn't know how long you'd be."

"You'd better go until I can get this mess sorted out."

I angle my cap farther down and take my time replacing my cleaning rags, so I have a chance to hear what she says next.

"What's going on?" Delta asks the Protector.

"If it's true that you have a son," the Protector says to Delta, "there's a good chance you'll be seeing him real soon. You!" She turns her attention back to me. "What are you waiting for? Get out."

As I move past Delta, she taps my wrist, and whispers urgently, "Get him out of here." Her head is turned away from the Protector when she speaks. I give her a brief nod before hurrying away. Unsure of my next move, I dart into the stairwell and slam the door behind me. I sink onto the top step and try to control my heart rate. I half expect to see Ghent. The Protector said they'd have him in custody soon, but maybe she was trying to scare Delta. If they had caught him, she would have said so. Ghent is fast, and good at hiding. He's going to be fine.

Chapter 16

Gripping my cleaning bucket so tight that my knuckles crack, I dart to the first floor. I open the door at the bottom of the stairwell a few inches and check the main corridor before charging past the spot where Gamma left me.

"Med-Tech Temple, please report to intensive care." The announcement blares over the intercom. I pick up the pace, making good time to the storage closet where I hurl the bucket of cleaning supplies inside before racing to the back door. I keep the uniform on, hitching up my trousers so I don't trip as I charge outside and slam the door behind me.

The air seems thicker now. The sun has reached its zenith, and I swelter under my double layer of clothing. I flip off the cap and use it to mop the sweat from my brow. Maybe I could stow the uniform in the rocks and get away incognito. If they're looking for anyone other than Ghent it will be a cleaner.

I dive behind the rocks, tearing at the buttons on the coveralls. My hands are trembling, and it takes way too long, but I finally work them loose. Yanking the uniform off, I crumple it into a bundle and press the cap on top. Then I shove the whole thing into a crevice between the boulders. It's not very well hidden, but hopefully no one will think to look out here anytime soon. The relative calm outside the Clinic scares me. It's almost too quiet.

Pressing my cheek against the warm boulder, I hug my knees to my chest and try to center myself. I have no idea where Ghent is, or if he can hear me, but I grab for the transmitter and hope for the best. My fingers come up empty. I pinch the rim of the collar and work my fingertips all the way around.

It's gone.

I can't stand up for fear that someone might see me, so I sit as straight as possible, clawing at my clothes and hoping the transmitter has simply slipped down inside the collar.

Nothing.

I scramble for it on hands and knees. Thinking it may have become snagged in the coveralls, I yank the bundle out from where I stashed it. Flattening the uniform on the ground, I pat my hands over every inch of it. The device isn't anywhere. I think back to my last clear memory of when I had it. I definitely had it with me in the intensive care unit. I remember it poking into my neck when I was pretending to clean the window frame. Could it have fallen into the bucket? That would mean Ghent might have heard Delta's warning.

I need to believe he heard her and that he's doing what she asked: escaping the palisade. At that thought, a hollow feeling churns through my stomach. If he's on his way out of here, I need to worry about myself. Stay out of sight. And I can't remain here. It's too close to the Clinic, and it's too exposed. What if I skirt around the fence-line to the far end of the reflection pool, near the woods where I first met Ghent? It's out of sight. It's well shaded, and there's water.

* * *

It only takes about ten minutes to get there. Everything looks so different from the other night. The sun blazes overhead and the leaves shimmer in the trees. The surface of the pool reflects the puffy clouds scattered across the sky. Resting my back against a sturdy tree trunk, my legs give out and I let myself slide to the ground. I'm completely exhausted. Whatever adrenaline I had in the Clinic has abandoned me. I should be scared, or hungry, but I feel nothing except blades of grass spearing into my open palms.

Leaning my head against the rough bark, I let out a breath and gaze across the pool. I have no idea how long I sit here, perfectly still, watching the water. Eventually, the sun begins its gradual shift toward the horizon. I wonder how long I can stay out here before Gamma starts to worry, or worse. Starts to search for me. So I push my shoulders into the tree trunk for leverage and force myself to my feet. I brush dirt from my trousers and glance around. It's quiet. The only smell is the sweet scent of the trees. That's when I hear it. A low breathy sound, coming from the other side of the reflection pool. Turning toward the noise, I creep through the underbrush to the other side of the water.

My heart skips a beat when I see him.

Ghent.

He's huddled between the roots of a gnarled oak, arms covered with grime, his shock of dark hair obscuring his features. His shoulders heave. Despite his bulk, he looks frail. He raises a forearm to wipe his eyes. That's when he notices me. He stares as if I'm a ghost, but he's the ghost. He should be gone by now. Before I can speak, he leaps to his feet and barrels into me, gripping me so tight I can hardly breathe.

"Ghent? What's wrong?"

He says nothing, just holds me, his chin draped over my shoulder, his embrace tightening around me, causing a stab of pain to shoot up my arm. I gasp, but he doesn't seem to notice. Finally, I wriggle to loosen his grip. He obliges, but doesn't let go of me fully, and doesn't raise his head. I allow myself to clasp the small of his back and rub in soft circles, feeling him relax under my palms.

"I'm so glad you're," he whispers into my hair. "I thought—"

"I'm fine." I gather the material of his shirt in my hands, surprised at how much I need to hold on to him.

Even though he's grimy and messed up, the scent of his mothers' lavender soap lingers on his skin. I allow myself to stroke his hair, organizing the ratty clumps into some semblance of order. He sighs. His facial fur grazes the side of my neck. I'm surprised to realize it doesn't bother me anymore.

We can't stay like this. I pry myself away and grip his upper arms.

"Ghent, you have to get out of here."

"I know."

Maintaining my grip, I push him to arms' length, marveling at how tall he is. I'm usually the tallest person in the room, but he towers over me. His face is a mess. I tentatively reach up to wipe the dirt from his cheeks. He lets me. Bolder now, I lick my thumb and wipe harder, like my mother used to do to me when I was a child. His skin is rough and hot. He raises his hand over mine and holds it there. His dark eyes are clearer now, the color of Ma Temple's hot chocolate, and they're fixed on mine.

Slowly, as if in a dream, he raises the back of a hand to my cheek and runs his knuckles across my jaw line. His touch is light as air. Surprising in its gentleness. I know this is wrong. I can't let him touch me. It's exactly what I was afraid of when I first met him. I look at my shoes, his mother's shoes, and pull away. He reaches up and grasps my chin, forcing me to face him. He tilts his head and examines me carefully. His expression is strong and vulnerable at the same time.

"Thank you," he says simply.

"For what?"

"Everything. I didn't really believe..." His breath hitches. "I never thought that a girl, a woman would help me, might even be my friend. My mothers warned me never to trust anyone, except them. And now you're here and you're perfect, and ... and we should stay together."

Something jolts inside of me. Part of me wants him to be right, but he isn't. Not in this life.

"We can't. You know that," I say. "And I'm far from perfect. I'm more of a monster than you ever were."

"Don't say that about yourself, Meg. Never say that." He slides his palm to cup my cheek. His skin is rough and warm against mine.

"I was wrong about so many things before, Ghent. I'm embarrassed about what I thought of you. But I understand now. I really do." I run my hand down his forearm and let it drop to my side. "I'm sorry about how I was before."

He takes a step back, releasing my face. I feel the loss of his closeness like a rush of cold air. I'm desperate to be closer to him, to hold him again, but we can't. He has to get out of here. "You heard what your mother said, right? You have to go."

He bows his head. "Goodbye, Meg."

He turns and begins to walk away without looking back. It's as if a tremendous weight is crushing my chest, stealing the air from my lungs. Even though I know it's the right thing to do, I can't let him go. Not like this.

"Wait," I call out, grabbing his arm and turning him to face me. I touch his cheek with the tips of my fingers. It's rough and furry, and warm. I slide my palm across the fur.

He glances at me, pupils dilating as he takes my free hand and brings it to the other side of his face. He tilts his head so that my fingertips cover his lips. Then he pulls my hand away from his mouth, turning it over in his palm so he can press a kiss to each of my knuckles in turn. A fire ignites inside me, a wonderful joined sensation I've never felt before.

And I want more.

I draw him closer and slide my fingers into his hair, pulling his face down so that our mouths collide. I've never done this before with anyone. Our noses bump, but we soon figure out how to arrange ourselves for optimum contact. This first kiss feels weird, but not in a bad way. In a strange way it feels right, more right than anything I could have imagined. Maybe this is the real reason I've never had a relationship with anyone inside the palisade. Perhaps I don't belong here anymore than Ghent does. Could it be true that we really do belong together? Should I go outside with him? Could I?

My thoughts melt away when his hands arc around my back to loosen my braid from its tie. His lips continue to explore my face. He plants tiny kisses on my eyelids, my cheeks, my nose, before returning to my lips. The grime on our skin mingles as his hands play through my hair. He unwinds my braid as I slip my hands under his shirt, reveling in the smooth skin stretched over hard muscle. I quiver as his hands start to move in expanding circles over my shoulders, finally catching his fingertips in my collar. This is all the reminder I need of the potential danger.

"Ghent." I try to push him away, but it takes more will than I bargained for. Neither of us wants to stop. "I lost the transmitter."

"I know." He moves in to press a kiss against my neck, right on the spot where the transmitter was planted.

"They could find it. They could find *you*."

His lips freeze against my neck. I shiver when he breaks contact. He places both hands on my shoulders and looks down at me, a sad smile playing over his features, top lip curving higher on the right side. Perfectly imperfect.

"You're sure you won't come with me?"

I want to. I want to so much that it hurts to say, "I can't." But that's what I make myself tell him.

"I guess this wasn't meant to be." He takes a step back, releasing me and drawing up to his full height. He reaches for his cloak where it hangs over a tree branch. He's truly leaving this time. A pang shoots through me.

"I'm not sorry we did that," he says, arranging the fabric across his shoulders.

"Me either." My entire body thrums with the need to hold him again, to follow him. But I force myself to stay where I am. If I let myself reach out for him, I'll never be able to let him go.

"I've always wondered what it would be like," he says.

Oh. My cheeks burn. It's not that he likes me. He was only curious. No wonder it was so easy for men to trick defenseless women into becoming Expectants, in the ancient times.

"Meg?" He looks horrified by my reaction. "Oh no, Meg."

He strides over and takes my hands, pulling them to his chest and wrapping them in one of his. Enfolding me in his arms, he draws his cloak around both of us, creating a perfect cocoon. "I'll never forget you. Whatever happens to me. You've changed my life." He pulls away and forces me to look at him. His eyes bore into mine and they're telling me hello and goodbye at the same time. He rests his forehead against mine and his words are a caress. "You'll always be my Meg."

Chapter 17

I don't know how I manage to let him go, but I do. My plan is to stay in the shadows for a few more hours, long enough for him to get outside the palisade. He's headed for an old gate in the palisade Delta told him about. It was part of their original plan. He wouldn't let me go there with him. Said there's too much open land, there would be too great a risk of my being spotted with him. So he left me at the reflection pool. I stare at the water until the sun begins to set, the hollow in my chest opening until I feel like it's going to swallow me whole. It's almost too dark to see the path when I finally pick my way back to the housing block.

As I walk, my mind replays the sensation of Ghent's lips on mine, the way his heart thumped strong and solid beneath my palm. Now he's gone. I pray he'll be safe out there. Hugging my arms around me, I quicken my pace as the sun's rays disappear from the sky, and my path is plunged into darkness, illuminated dimly by solar-powered lamps. I can't see much by their light: only a few clumps of flowers growing wild beside the pathway and the smoke puffing from the factory's chimney in the distance.

Eventually, the lights of the housing block come into view. A handful of workers straggle home from the factories and the fields. Life goes on. The lights are on in the Temples' quarters. Gamma's probably waiting for me. Her mother could be there too, but it's a chance I'll have to take. Slipping to the side entrance, I'm confronted by a shadowy figure on the stoop, knees clutched to her chest. Her head snaps up when I came into view.

"Omega?"

It's Gamma. She doesn't move, even when I take a hesitant step closer. She's not looking at me at all. She's staring into the distance.

"What's wrong?" I ask.

Her face is pale, eyes wide and lost. I crouch in front of her, reaching slowly to touch her knee. A few women have wandered up the path. Not wanting them to hear us, I pull Gamma to her feet and drag her away from the stoop. She lets me move her without protest. Her shoulders slump as we wait for the women to pass. One dumps a cigarette butt in the dirt before she goes inside the housing block.

I grasp Gamma's wrists. Her skin is icy. "What's going on?"

"They weren't just rumors," she says. "*Demen* are real. Real people. And my mom is a murderer." Her voice cracks on the last word.

"Tell me what this is about." My fingers dig into her forearms as I will her to focus.

"It's true. Delta and Epsilon have a son." She pulls free and wipes her cheeks roughly with her knuckles. "*Had* a son."

"Gamma, please." My heart thuds. I drag her farther from the building so we're out of earshot of anyone who might pass by on their way home.

"Delta and Epsilon's *son,*" she says. "He came for them. Did you see him? My mother made me stay in her office, but I heard everything. She left her comm channel open. I heard everything. He was real. He was a real person. Like us."

She drops to her knees and I sink down beside her.

"What happened?" I ask.

"He's dead," she says. "My mother killed him."

A chill descends over me. No. Ghent's not dead. He escaped the palisade. I reach for Gamma but she shoves me away and rises to her feet, turning away from the housing block. I follow, catching up easily, and I grab her elbow. She rounds on me. "He was real. And Mom's a killer, a hired hand for the Protectors."

"Please. Tell me."

"Delta and Epsilon's son. He came to the Clinic. To turn himself in." Her eyes glisten in the moonlight.

"No, he got away." It's a risk to reveal I know even this much, but she doesn't seem to notice my slip.

"Yes, he got away." She pauses. "The first time."

What?

"The first time he went to the Clinic he planted some kind of listening device in his mothers' room. The Med-Techs found a transmitter on the floor beside the bed."

So that's what happened to the transmitter. I dropped it. In his mothers' room.

"Why would he do that?" I ask, knowing that he didn't do it at all. It was me.

"To monitor his birth mother's condition," Gamma says. An image of Epsie plays in my mind. So like her son. Tousled brown hair and deathly pale skin. "He knew what was wrong with her, that there was only one chance to make her better. It was actually quite brave. That's when I realized. He was a person. Just like us. He did exactly what I'd do to save someone I love."

She grabs my hand as if it's a lifeline.

"None of this makes sense," I say.

"No, it doesn't," Gamma said. "If he could get into their room, why didn't he talk to them? Why only plant a transmitter? The Protectors think he might have done it remotely, like through a vent or something." Gamma's missed my point. And anyway I know exactly how the transmitter got there. "He was listening in, you see. He heard my mom talking with his mom, trying to convince her that the only chance to save her partner was a kidney transplant from a blood relative."

"And Delta suggested they find her son?" I ask, horrified at the betrayal.

"No. She kept her mouth shut even after Mom told her that her partner could die. She wouldn't even admit that the child existed."

"Then how did he..." My words catch in my throat as I realize exactly what must have happened. Ghent overheard the conversation and decided to turn himself in, to sacrifice himself to save Epsie. I think back to how he was at the reflection pool. When he said goodbye he knew he wasn't escaping the palisade. He was going to sacrifice himself to the Protectors. He wouldn't let me go with him to the gate because he wasn't going there himself.

"What happened after that?" I say.

"Not long after their conversation, the *deman* showed up at the Clinic. Snuck in the back way as if he didn't want to cause a panic."

He didn't.

"That's when Mom locked me away in her office," Gamma continues, puffing a lock of hair from her mouth. "She had to go and perform the transplant." Gamma's voice hitches. "Then she killed him. By lethal injection. I heard one of those Protectors authorize it."

I barely make out her last words. I'm already running. As far and as fast as my legs will carry me.

Chapter 18

I tear down the path to the open field, stumbling over loose gravel. Gamma doesn't follow. I run until I can't run anymore, my breath catching in ragged gasps, hair streaming in all directions.

He's not dead.

He can't be.

My feet instinctively follow his directions to the wall, the gate Delta told him about. When I see it, a scream rips through my lungs. The gate is here. Exactly where it's supposed to be. It hasn't been touched. Not in eons by the looks of it. It's covered with brambles. No one has passed through here in a long time. Gamma was right. Ghent didn't come here. He went to the Clinic.

The back of my throat is raw. The massive stone wall looms over me, at least twenty feet high, smaller rocks piled on larger boulders. There are said to be huge iron spikes on the other side to protect us from the *demen*. It's the *demen* who need protection from us.

I pummel the wall until my hands are bruised and bloody. Naturally, the stone doesn't yield. I press my whole body into it and sink to the ground, clawing at the rock, seeding it with my blood. In this moment, I know I need to leave. I have to get outside the palisade.

But there's something else I need to do first.

Blood trickles between my fingers as I walk in the direction of the Clinic. Its gate is open as always. *All those in need are welcome here.* The entrance is illuminated by solar panels. I approach with determined steps down the cobblestone path, shoving the glass doors open and striding into the waiting area. There's a solitary Aide at the desk: a mousy woman, pale and tired-looking. I must seem horrific to her with my mutant eyes in plain sight, ripped clothes and bloodied hands. I don't care.

"Do you have an appointment?"

I'm almost impressed that she manages to retain her professional façade. I ignore her and push through the inner doors.

"Wait! You can't go in there."

The lights in the corridor lead me to the stairwell. I climb to the second floor. To intensive care. Room two-one-three. No guard today.

Epsie's bed is empty, the machines unplugged, wires and tubes draped over the bedhead like coiled snakes. Delta's chair has been placed against the far wall. But the room isn't empty. A black clad figure stands by the window. Her head is bent over a small metal object that she holds between her thumb and forefinger.

Ghent's transmitter.

She glances up. "Daughter Wye, I wondered when you'd be making an appearance." Her features are arranged in the same sneer I remember from our last encounter. Then it sent chills through me. Now, I have to force myself to hold still, to keep my hands by my sides.

"Interesting technology," she remarks. "Did you help him make it?"

This is why he's gone. Because I was stupid enough to drop the transmitter. That's why he heard what Ma Temple said to Delta, why he's dead. My clumsiness sealed his fate. I wish I could re-do this day. I should be punished for my carelessness. I held Ghent's life in my hands, and I threw it away. The best way to punish myself is obvious.

I go straight for the commander, grasping for the transmitter and clawing at her face. She's taller and stronger than me, but she doesn't expect it. I manage to drive her to the window and hold her there, fingers wrapped around her throat before she gets her bearing and shoves me to the ground. The transmitter clatters to the floor. I reach for it, but her boot crashes down on my hand. I whimper. She grinds her heel into my hand. More pain spikes through my fingers, but I don't cry out. I deserve this. She lifts her foot and I think she's going to kick me, but instead she nudges me aside with her toe as she bends to collect the transmitter. I struggle to my knees, clutching my hand to my chest.

"Now, Daughter Wye. There's no need for this." I'm gratified that her voice is a little shaky. Her hair is mussed, and she wipes her cheek, gaping at the blood my fingernails have drawn. I try to get my feet beneath me, but she strides over and presses me back down. "You're fine right there," she says. I'm waiting for her to call for back up, but she doesn't. Instead, she collects the chair and places it in front of me. When she sits, her breath is already under control, even though I'm still winded. She runs her thumb over the transmitter before slipping it into her pocket.

"Why?" The syllable escapes on a ragged breath. I bite down on my lip to stop it from quivering.

The commander seems to be talking to herself when she says, "Neither of us got what we wanted."

I don't understand why she's not more triumphant. She's won. The *deman* is gone.

"You killed him." The words take some effort. "He was only trying to help his mother. And you killed him."

The corner of her mouth turns down. "I wouldn't expect you to understand. You of all people." She turns to the window, apparently losing interest in me.

I rise to my feet. She doesn't stop me this time. Even though she's facing me again now, it's as if she doesn't see me as she spits on her palm to clean the blood from her hands.

"Where are they?" I ask, pointing to the empty bed.

I don't expect an answer so I'm surprised when I get one. "In recovery," she says. "His birth mother survived the surgery."

I lunge for the door, hoping to remember the location of the recovery room. I think it's on the first floor. The commander's voice freezes me. "At least you won't be the one having his babies. Your bloodline is sullied enough."

"I never wanted his *babies*. I only wanted him to be safe. As far away from us as he could get."

Now I know the truth. She's the real monster here. She could have stood by my mother, but she chose to reject her. She could have been loved, but she chose hatred. I hope it kills her slowly from the inside. Looking at her now, I think it might. I shut the door behind me and don't look back.

Chapter 19

No one approaches me as I make my way to the recovery room. I suppose I look like a patient with my messed-up hands. I keep moving to avoid unwanted attention. Through the glass wall of the recovery room, I can see several beds lined up in a row. Only one of them is occupied.

Epsie.

She's unconscious, but she has more color than she did earlier. Delta sits beside her, brushing the hair back from her forehead and murmuring in her ear. A Protector is stationed on the other side of the bed engrossed in something on her datapad. I want to go inside, to talk to Delta. I need to know Epsie will live, that Ghent didn't sacrifice himself for nothing. But what can I say to them? If it weren't for me, their son would be alive. Far away from here.

And Epsie would be dead, I remind myself.

Delta glances at the Protector and mutters something. The guard nods, turning her attention back to the datapad. Delta rises and brushes off her clothing. Collecting an empty glass from the cabinet beside the bed, she makes for the door. She looks terrible, pale skin and sunken cheeks. *This is all my fault.*

When she sees me, she freezes in place, eyes fixing on mine through the glass.

She approaches from the other side of the partition. I panic. This was a stupid idea. I'm the reason her son is dead. I bolt down the hallway Gamma led me through earlier, past the closet where I tossed my cleaning bucket, all the way to the exit. Slamming the door behind me.

Again I'm running. Just like before. No clear destination. Only escape, pure and simple. Escape from myself. Eventually, my feet take me to the reflection pool. Where Ghent said goodbye. The water reflects the now-starry sky. An owl hoots in the distance. It's eerily peaceful. I drop to my knees and try to call to mind every detail of Ghent's face. The color of his eyes, the asymmetric tilt of his lips. Someone should remember. Someone other than his family. He existed. He was a person and he was here. Even though he wasn't meant to be.

A small metallic object glints under the moonlight, in the grass. I reach for it. It's smooth and cool, and familiar: the receiver for Ghent's transmitter. He must have left it here. After he heard what Ma Temple said to Delta. I can visualize him sitting where I am now, turning her words over in his mind. Making his decision. Did he think I'd try to stop him if he told me the truth? Or was he afraid I wouldn't try? I hold the device against my cheek, letting a single tear wash over it.

Twigs rustle behind me and a dark figure emerges from the trees. Did someone follow me from the Clinic? I scan the woman from the ground up. She's tall. Wearing dark trousers and a long-sleeved shirt, a cloak draped over her arm. Her dark hair is pulled back into a messy ponytail.

"Omega?" She takes a step closer.

I blink in disbelief.

"Mom?"

She runs over and gathers me in her arms. How is she here? She holds me tight, smoothing my hair. Her heart thumps loud and true beneath my ear.

"It's going to be alright," she says. She smells of woodlands and fresh air. Her long hair is swept back from her face. She feels like home.

"What are you doing here?"

I allow her to guide me to a fallen log where she pulls me down beside her and loops her cloak over my shoulders. I slip Ghent's transmitter into my pocket.

"I'm so sorry, honey. I should have been here. I was worried something like this might happen, but there were things I needed to do."

I fall into her, allowing her to cradle my head against her shoulder.

"Do you want to tell me about what's happened?" She plucks at a strand of hair plastered to my tear-stained cheek.

How can I tell her any of this? Now that I know what that *deman* did to her all those hundreds of weeks ago. She couldn't possibly understand about Ghent.

"Mom, I know about what happened to you. Before I was born."

The hand she had pressed against my cheek tenses. "Ma Temple told you." It's a statement, not a question. She drops her elbows to her knees and looks off into the distance. "I'm sorry I wasn't the one to explain. I understand if you're angry. I shouldn't have kept it from you."

I notice her communicator is missing from her wrist.

"Honey, there's a lot I have to tell you. But we need to wait a few moments. We're expecting company. She shouldn't be long."

"Who?"

Mom begins to rearrange my hair around my shoulders, straightening out some of the tangles.

"A new ally, I hope," she says. "Before we get into all that, are you really okay?"

"Did Omicron call you back? What did she tell you?"

"I know you fell into something that should never have been your burden to carry. Please talk to me, honey."

I'm actually surprised at how easy it is once I start talking. The words spill out. She doesn't interrupt. Her expression darkens when I tell her about my encounter with Commander Theta. I spare her some of the details. They loved each other once. When I'm done, Mom rests her hands on either side of my face. Her skin smells of the woods and the fields. Her cloak slips to the ground, but neither of us moves to retrieve it. Her emerald eyes glint in the moonlight. The color that matches exactly one of mine.

She stares up at the sky for a few moments before she says, "I suppose I should fill you in on a few things while we're waiting. You need to know what really happened the first time I went outside the palisade, the whole story."

"The first time?" I say.

"Ma Temple told you about how the Protectors found me, I suppose? With the emergency beacon?"

I nod, but I don't understand what this has to do with anything.

"The thing is, I never activated that beacon. I didn't even bring it with me when I left the palisade. I went out exploring without thinking it through. I had to know what was out there. I couldn't bear for Theta and me to start a family of our own, without knowing. Our society won't last like this forever. I couldn't bring a child into the palisade without knowing there would be a bigger world for her to live in, that she wouldn't die out with everyone else imprisoned inside these stone walls. I needed to know there would be more for her. For you."

Her eyes narrow. "When that man took me..." she starts.

"You don't have to tell me." I reach for her hand, but she waves me away and keeps talking as if she won't get through it if she lets herself stop.

"He held me in a cave for a while, but eventually, he left me there alone." It's hard to believe she's talking about my biological father. "I must have passed out. The next thing I remember, the sun was setting and I was being carried to a clearing about fifty yards from the palisade. There were voices. Arguing around me. Concerned they were getting too close, that it wouldn't be safe, but the man carrying me—"

"Another man?"

"Yes, a gentle soul. Your Ghent sounds a little like him." *My Ghent*. A dark hollow in my chest cracks open as my mother continues. "He settled me on the ground and tucked my cloak around me. He pressed an emergency beacon into my arms and activated it. I don't know where he got it. He waited with me until he was sure the signal had been received, and then he disappeared. That's how I know we're not alone. There are people out there. Men and woman. Some of the voices I heard out there were women. I'm sure of it."

"Why you didn't tell me any of this before?"

"I didn't think you were ready."

"You said you've been outside more than once. When? Where we you really this week?"

A twig crackles behind us and I glance around as my mother whispers, "We can't talk about that yet, but I'll explain soon. I promise."

Another shaded figure emerges at the edge of the trees.

"Sigma?" A familiar voice calls for my mother, sending a chill through my veins. *Ma Temple*. I can make out her white scrubs against the darkness. She's holding something by her side. A Med-Kit? She killed Ghent and now she's come for me and my mother. I shoot to my feet and launch myself at her, but something pulls me aside. My mother has me by the arm.

"Omega, it's alright," Mom says.

"Mom! Weren't you listening to me? She killed Ghent. She's working with them. It's not safe."

She grips my shoulders and turns me to face her. "Yes, it is honey. She's with me. With us. We have a plan."

Ma Temple hasn't moved from her position at the edge of the clearing. Finally she speaks. "Omega, I'm not your enemy. Please believe that." She takes a single step forward. I flinch.

"What's the Med-Kit for?" I ask. "More lethal injections?"

My mother's grip tightens around me. "She's here to help, honey. I asked if she'd mind patching up your bruises before we get moving." She glances at Ma Temple and a strange look passes between them. "Would it be alright if she takes a look?" My mother maneuvers me back to the log, and I let her press me down to a sitting position. I'm exhausted and confused. My mother nods at Ma Temple who approaches cautiously, keeping her hands by her sides as she kneels in front of me. She deposits the Med-Kit on the ground and flicks a small flashlight on, leaning it against the log, angled so she can see me better.

"I'll keep watch," Mom says, squeezing my shoulder before taking a few paces away. Ma Temple fumbles with the clasp on the Med-Kit. I soon realize it's because her hands are shaking. She finally manages to open it and retrieves a syringe and a vial of clear fluid. She holds it up to show me.

"It's only an anesthetic with a mild sedative. I can work without it, but it will make you more comfortable." She doesn't move any closer, waiting for my response.

"It's okay, honey," Mom says, as she takes a few paces around the clearing checking our surroundings. "Let Ma Temple help you, and then we'll get going."

"Going where?"

"To see an old friend," Mom says. She smiles at me.

When I nod to Ma Temple, she lets out a breath and unseals an alcohol swab. She moves slowly, looking up into my face periodically to check that I'm comfortable. She begins to cleanse my skin before inserting the needle. I hardly feel it, and soon a warm sensation floods through me, making me feel light all over.

"Better?" she asks as she leans in close, expertly examining each of my hands before turning her attention to the sutures in my arm. Some of them appear to have torn during my tussle with the commander. Ma Temple selects the equipment she needs from the Med-Kit and sets to work removing the damaged stitches and replacing them with her own, glancing at my mother every now and again. For her part, Mom seems to be doing a pretty professional job of patrolling the clearing. Like she's done this before. I can feel the tug of Ma Temple's needle against my skin and try to focus anywhere but on my arm. My thoughts are beginning to drift. It must be the affects of the anesthetic. I'm still not a hundred percent sure about Ma Temple, but I trust my Mom, and she said to let Ma Temple work on me.

Of course, Ma Temple's hair is perfectly French-braided around the crown of her head. I notice this as she bends over the Med-Kit. She unwraps some more alcohol swabs, a lot more, and rubs them carefully over each of my fingers and around each wrist. "I don't think anything is broken." I wince at her touch. "Perhaps a hairline fracture here. It will mend on its own easily enough."

She sifts through the sticking plasters in the kit and picks out some that are the right size for my worst cuts. When she's done, she starts to pack up, organizing each item carefully in the small case.

She extinguishes the light and makes that clucking sound in the back of her throat. Mom turns around.

"All done?" she says. "How are you feeling, sweetheart?"

The injection has taken away most of the physical pain. Now I feel heavy and tired. The scent of the woods reminds me of Ghent, but I'm too tired to even think about him. Something heavy and warm drapes around me and I realize Mom has slipped her cloak over my shoulders again.

"Honey?" She eyes me with concern.

"I'm okay." My voice sounds like it's coming from far away.

"What did you give her?" my mother asks Ma Temple, her voice laced with anxiety. "We need to explain everything and she can barely stand up."

"It was only a mild sedative, Sigma. She's dead on her feet. She needs rest."

"I wish we had time for that. Can we get her to the transport like this?" My mother props me against her shoulder and tries to lift me. I stagger to her side.

"Wait." A nasty thought pierces the haze of my brain. "We can't go back to our quarters. Theta has a guard posted there."

"Don't worry, honey. That's not where we're going." My

mother's breath puffs warm against my cheek. She's speaking to Ma Temple now. "Help me get her to the path."

I feel a jolt on my other side as Ma Temple and Mom brace me between them.

"Where are we going?" I ask.

"It's not much farther." My mother's words are the last thing I hear before my muscles give out and darkness claims me.

Chapter 20

A bump startles me awake, knocking my teeth together. I'm curled up in a snug space pressed against someone's side. Something warm and soft has been draped over my legs. The person beside me is massaging my arms in gentle comforting strokes. Everything's so warm and soft. I must be dreaming. The jostling increases. I force my eyes open to relative darkness. The first thing I see is my mother's concerned expression. I'm curled against her side in the back of an electric vehicle.

"Are you okay?" Her arm is around my shoulders. I can make out the back of Ma Temple's French braid in the front passenger seat.

"Everything good back there?" The driver's voice is familiar too. Private Upsilon.

I press my knuckles against my temple. "What's going on?"

"We'll explain when we get there." My mother rubs my arm again.

In contrast to Ma Temple's rigid posture, Upsilon's shoulders are relaxed. I try to figure out where we are, but it's difficult to see much from the back, particularly at night. The lights of the housing block flicker dimly to our right, but we're heading away from them.

"Kill the lights," Ma Temple says, leaning toward Upsilon.

Upsilon presses a button in the front panel to extinguish the headlights. My mother leans back and reties her ponytail at the nape of her neck, gathering the stray strands together in the process. The vehicle slows as we drive on in near-darkness. We approach a dimly lit single-story building made of pale cream stone that glints in the moonlight. I've never seen it before but I know what it is. The Elders' private quarters. No one comes here without an invitation, and invitations are rare from what I understand. Upsilon pulls around to the side and stops beside a recessed opening in the exterior wall.

"Everything will be fine, Omega." Mom pats my wrist as Upsilon and Ma Temple swing their doors open and glide from their seats into the darkness. Mom guides me by the arm and Upsilon steadies me once I'm outside the vehicle. I'm still a little woozy.

The air is rich with the scent of gardenias. The same fragrance I recall from when Omicron stopped Theta interrogating me at the Nest. That seems like a lifetime ago. I lurch to the side and Upsilon grabs for me while Ma Temple snaps on a flashlight. Upsilon braces me with an arm around my waist before my mother pushes her away and guides me forward. I notice in the flashlight beam that my mother's skin is a little darker than when she left, as if she's been out in the sun, not in a retreat. I try to speak, but my mother shushes me, pointing at a recessed door ahead of us.

I hear the soft purr of the electric vehicle as it starts up and slowly fades into the distance. That's when I notice Upsilon is gone. It's only me, my mother, and Ma Temple now. My mother guides me to the entryway and places a thumb into a well-concealed panel. The door opens. *Biometric locks?* That's highly specialized tech. Why are the Elders' quarters coded to accept my mom's fingerprints?

The three of us hurry into some kind of service entrance that opens to a narrow hallway. The walls are dark brown with a fluorescent bar along the ceiling. We hurry across the stone-tiled floor. The space is almost clinically clean, no dust anywhere, and the corridor is so narrow we have to walk single file. Mom goes first, with me in the middle and Ma Temple behind me. I can't say her presence gives me much comfort. A lemony scent permeates the air. It reminds me of the detergent we use in the factory. After about twenty feet, we get to a wood-paneled door. Mom opens it and ushers me into a circular atrium with a domed glass ceiling. Moonlight streams through to illuminate potted plants in handcrafted ceramic tubs and stacks of cushions organized around the edges of the polished timber floor. This must be where the Elders meditate. Several more wood-paneled doors are evenly spaced around the perimeter of the room. Ma Temple moves toward one of them.

"Sigma, we should hurry," she says.

Mom motions for me to follow. She opens the door and ushers us through. It self-locks behind us.

We're in a larger hallway now. The walls are painted burgundy, the floor covered with a thick pile carpet. I glance at my mother, surprised by the determined set of her jaw. The hallway is illuminated by ornate lamps spaced at regular intervals. Interspersed between them are screens displaying images of the past. Most of them are in shades of gray, with the occasional color picture interrupting the pattern. I slow down to get a better look. They depict horrors from the ancient wars. Familiar scenes from history class: burned buildings, abandoned cityscapes, people bleeding in the streets, men and women, dying and suffering. Together. There's something peculiar about the surfaces of the images, grainy and imperfect. Suddenly, I realize where I've seen pictures like this before, or rather one picture. Ghent's photograph of his mothers. These are much larger in scale, but the same tech.

Lost in the details, I fail to keep pace with the others. I'm startled when Ma Temple turns back for me, clasping her hands at her waist. "Horrifying, aren't they?" She glides behind me to look over my shoulder at the picture I've been examining. I flinch at her proximity but she ignores me, apparently lost in the image: a woman shielding a baby from something in the distance. The infant is wrapped in a dirty blanket, the woman's face streaked with dirt and tears.

"Why are these here?" I ask.

"To remind us of what was. So it never happens again. Those who forget the past are doomed to repeat it." Ma Temple says.

"We won't be repeating any mistakes once we all die out," Mom says, taking a few steps toward us.

Ma Temple's shoulders straighten and it looks like she's about to respond. I get the feeling this isn't the first time they've had this argument. But when she speaks, she only says, "We need to keep moving." She turns and walks away. It's difficult to tear myself away from the photograph, but when I finally do, I don't want to look back. I can't bear it.

Eventually, we stop at a plain wooden door. Mom presses her thumb against a panel beside it and the door opens to a miniature version of the atrium outside, except this room is carpeted, the same plush carpet as the hallway. While the walls are curved, they are not completely spherical. In place of the glass panel in the ceiling, this room has a tinted picture window on the far wall. The sun is rising, and I can make out the silhouettes of gardenias in the dull purple light. Birds are beginning to chirp outside.

The walls are painted in mute colors and there is little in the way of furniture – only a low wooden bench with cushions on the floor around it. The side wall houses several smaller doors. One of them opens without warning, causing me to jerk back against my mother. Two figures emerge. One is Omicron, her dark robes cinched with a crimson tie. Her gray hair flows over her shoulders, as she leans against her cane, and bows her head to acknowledge us. The other woman is younger, tall and thin, with blonde hair and ice-blue eyes. She's wearing a loose-fitting crimson robe. Though her face is puffy and red, she looks more serene than when I last saw her: Delta.

Chapter 21

When Delta catches sight of us she stiffens. I'm tempted to turn and run. I don't know what to say to her. My knees begin to buckle, but my mother holds me steady.

Omicron addresses Mom, "Welcome back, my child. It's so good to see you again. And all in one piece, too." In a flash, my mother is across the room and drops to her knees in front of the Elder, holding the older woman's hand to her cheek.

"I failed," she whispers. "I let you down."

Omicron pulls Mom to her feet and places a hand over her own heart. "You could never disappoint me, child."

It's such an intimate moment. After a while, Mom turns to Delta and clasps her forearms gently. "I'm sorry."

They know each other too? All this time, Ghent's mother was friends with my Mom, and I never even knew he existed.

"Thank you for seeing us at short notice." Ma Temple bows before the Elder, drawing attention to herself. Not knowing what to do, I try to imitate her movement and almost overbalance in the process. I feel Ma Temple's steadying grip on my arm. When I raise my head, Delta's staring at Ma Temple, the flush of anger unmistakable in her cheeks. I pull out of Ma Temple's grip, worried Delta will think I'm working with her. Then I realize that I am working with her.

Omicron continues as if this is a perfectly ordinary gathering. "It's my pleasure, and I do believe this is the right time." She turns to Delta. "If you wouldn't mind, Healer." Delta places her fingertips beneath Omicron's elbow and guides her forward. The hem of her robe swishes around bare ankles as they move. They stop in the center of the room where Delta assists Omicron to sit on the bench. Mom follows and stands by the Elder's side.

Omicron places her cane flat on the seat beside her, and regards us all, her fingers tented beneath her chin. "Please sit."

She indicates the cushions at our feet. Delta sinks down on the one closest to Omicron, tucking her legs beneath her. Mom hurries over to me and helps me to my own cushion, taking her place on the floor beside it. Ma Temple sits on the other side of my mom, as far away from Delta as she can get.

Omicron bends forward to examine my bandaged fingers. "Seems like you've had another busy day."

I don't know if she's joking, so I don't respond. I tuck my bandaged hands into the folds of my shift.

Delta has remained silent this whole time, watching us. I turn to her and finally speak the words I should have offered her at the Clinic. "I'm so sorry. About Ghent." His name sticks in my throat. "I know he died because of me."

Delta opens her mouth to respond, but Omicron interrupts. "Let's not get ahead of ourselves," she says. "Perhaps we should start at the beginning. I want to thank you all for coming here. The things we discuss today must be kept private. While I am not completely alone amongst the Elders in harboring certain concerns, I am in a rather small minority. Until more of us feel this way, it is important that we conduct our business in relative secrecy. Unfortunate, but necessary. I know this may be frightening for you, child"—she turns to me—"but it is of great importance. This may take some time to explain. Are you comfortable?"

I nod, embarrassed by my ungainly position on the cushion. My legs are stiff and sore, making it hard to sit like the others.

"Perhaps you would like to take off your shoes?" Omicron's invitation is very tempting but I'm wearing Epsie's shoes and I'd be too embarrassed to flaunt them in front of Delta.

"No thanks. I'm fine." I attempt to reorganize myself into a less awkward position with my feet curled beneath me, concealing the boots.

"Our time is limited, but we need to start at the beginning so the child understands what we're asking of her." Omicron pinches her brow with a gnarled finger and suddenly keels over coughing. Deep throaty heaves rasp from her chest.

Delta's arm darts out to steady her as Mom screams, "Mother!" Mom races to the Elder's side and kneels, grasping her shoulders and steadying her until the coughing dies down. When they both look up, everyone is staring at them and my mother clamps a hand over her mouth. Omicron takes a minute to catch her breath before dropping her hand to Mom's shoulder and smiling.

"I suppose that is one thing we no longer have to explain," Omicron says. My mother's face is ashen, but Omicron chuckles. "Daughter, in the larger scheme of things, the fact that these women have learned you are my child is the least of our worries."

"But Elders don't have children," I say.

"This one does, my granddaughter." Omicron seems somewhat amused by the reaction to her revelation. "Simply believe that I love you and am proud of you. Both. However, the story of our family is for another time. What is important now is that you understand the choice we will ask you to make, and why we are asking it of you."

The sun's rays begin to peek through the window. Ma Temple glances at her communicator. "Yes, Healer." Omicron acknowledges the concern. "Time is short, and we must press on." The Elder makes a motion with her hand to indicate that Ma Temple should speak now.

Gamma's mother casts a furtive glance at Delta who is glaring at her as if she would like to kill her. Not surprising. Ma Temple took her child away. Forever. I grip my elbows in my palms, as I remember Ghent's quirky smile, his lips against mine. All gone now.

"Omega," Ma Temple interrupts my thoughts. "How much do you know about the Procedure?"

"Only what we learned in school."

"You didn't tell her anything?" Ma Temple glares at my

mother who ignores her and wraps a protective arm around my shoulders. "Great work for someone who believes we're letting our society go extinct because of our ignorance." My mother's arm tenses, but she makes no retort. Ma Temple returns her attention to me. "Do you know anything about natural reproduction?"

"You mean in the days before the Procedure?" I shuffle back on my cushion, grateful for my mother's arm.

Omicron's gaze shifts between Ma Temple and my mother, brows raised. "Perhaps there is an easier way to approach this?"

Everyone is looking at me, even Delta. Her fingers, which have been threading through the belt of her robe, have come to rest in her lap.

Omicron clutches the end of her cane, rolling it along the bench beside her. It makes a rattling sound. "Omega, you know why the palisade was originally built?"

The words come out automatically, the familiar litany we're taught at school. "To protect women from *demen*." My cheeks flush when I realize what I've just said, how offensive if must have sounded to Delta. But when I look at her, she's gazing out the window where a blue-jay hops along a tree branch.

"Yes and no," Omicron continues. "Did you know that it wasn't only women to begin with? Some men were here too, at first. They saw that the human race was tearing itself apart. In order for the species to survive, something needed to be done. The women needed to be protected. People were being killed faster than they could be born. The men who dreamed of a better future built the palisade to protect their families. Some of the first children born inside the wall were boys."

I grip my cushion tight, ignoring the pain in my bandaged fingers. This is not what they teach us at school.

"It's true, dear," Omicron says. "The first few generations here comprised both men and women, reproducing naturally. No Procedure. Eventually, fears grew that the new society would revert to the old ways, that the men would become powerful and greedy again, turn against each other, and put everyone at risk."

"The men were driven out?" I ask.

"Not immediately," Omicron says. "The older men gradually died off. Some went off to hunt and explore outside the walls, to see if the lands had improved since the wars. Many never returned. Those that did come back shared rumors of new societies developing outside the walls, building their own tools and hunting their own food. The rumors prompted others to try their luck outside, seeking a less retrained life than what they found inside the palisade. Those left inside were fearful of what would happen if another male-dominated society grew too strong outside. The risks it would mean for those inside.

After much discussion, the leaders decided that as long as the palisade was secure, it would be better not to repeat the mistakes of the past, to leave those who ventured outside to their own devices. Let those outside take their own risks. If the wars started again out there, at least the people sheltered within the walls would be safe. More than that, they decided that a society comprised only of women would be less risky for all of those inside the walls. Less aggressive impulses, you see, at least that was the theory. No one ultimately objected when the Med-Techs set up a plan to genetically engineer all children to be girls."

I want to ask what it took to get the men to agree to this, how many were even left inside the palisade at the time, and what happened to those who stayed. But before I can speak, Omicron is overcome by another coughing fit. My mother rushes from the room and returns a few moments later with a glass of water. She leans over Omicron and helps her drink.

"Thank you, my child." Omicron beckons that Mom should resume her seat on the cushion, before placing the glass down on the bench beside her. "Perhaps you could take over from here?" Omicron nods to Ma Temple.

"Omega, even after the men were gone, we still needed male

genetic material to breed." Ma Temple is running her fingernails through the carpet. "For generations, we were able to use frozen genetic material donated by the original male inhabitants and stored in a secure facility. It's called the Bank." She pauses and looks to Omicron who is sipping at her water.

Ma Temple speaks again, hesitantly, as if the words are being pulled from her against her will. "Few people know about the Bank. Most of the Med-Techs don't even know where the genetic material comes from. They send a requisition when they need it. In recent generations, we've had some problems. We think it's because the stored genetic material eventually degrades. This has led to unsuccessful implantations and abnormalities."

"That's why the population has stopped growing?" I ask.

My mother speaks up, and this time her words make a horrible kind of sense. "We're dying out, and it's not only genetic material. We don't have enough left in the stores from the days before the palisade. Some of it we can replace ourselves but a lot will soon be gone for good. We need to take steps."

Omicron raises a hand. She looks tired. I hadn't noticed the dark circles beneath her eyes earlier. But despite the fatigue in her face, I can see the resemblance to my mother: the green eyes with high arched brows, and the olive skin.

Omicron motions for my mother to sit back down as she raises the rim of her glass to her lips. The room descends into silence while we wait for her to drink. When she replaces the glass on the bench, she says, "It's obvious we won't solve the shortages today, and we have more pressing matters to discuss. Suffice to say, through my daughter's efforts and those of some others I cannot yet name, we know enough about the outside to believe it's more than a wasteland."

"But I didn't find it, Mother," my mom addresses Omicron, her tone dripping with defeat. "I still haven't found any trace of the sanctuary."

Ma Temple huffs and crosses her arms over her chest. "That's because it doesn't exist."

My mother ignores her and continues speaking to Omicron. "I didn't get any farther than the stream before you called me back."

"It's true?" I turn to Mom. "You were outside this week?"

"She only did as I requested," Omicron says as she glances at Delta. "I had a feeling we would be needing more information about the outside sooner rather than later."

A muscle twitches in Delta's jaw, reminding me again of her son. My heart squeezes at the thought of him.

"Omega, you need to know the rest," my mother says. "Then you can decide if you want to help us."

Help them? Delta remains silent, tears dripping from her eyes. She doesn't wipe them away. Omicron places a hand to her cheek, and Delta drops her head, letting the tears splash to the floor, absorbing into the carpet. Ma Temple clears her throat before turning her attention back to me. My mother is silent at my side as Ma Temple speaks again. "Omega, you know that we can genetically engineer a child for certain physical characteristics: eye color, hair color, and the like?"

"That's why you couldn't do anything about my eyes. It was too late to control for the mutation."

Her next words tumble out in a rush. "You have to understand, we're not proud of what we've done."

"What do you mean?" I ask.

"We can create male children. We *have* created male children."

"You mean like Delta and Epsie did?" I ask.

"That was an accident. We do it on purpose." Ma Temple evades my gaze.

"Why? If you create male children, where are they?" And suddenly I understand. "They're in the Bank, aren't they? You use them for new genetic material?"

Nobody answers.

"How could you?" I say. "You're using them, like breeding

stock!"

When Ma Temple responds, her voice is hoarse. "We only make as many as we need. We keep them safe and comfortable. We wouldn't have done it if there was any other way."

"And it has created some unexpected opportunities," Omicron says as she leans over to brush away Delta's tears. Not for the first time, I wonder why Delta is here. The others, I can understand. They're on some crazy mission to break outside the palisade and reintroduce *demen* into the population. They're all in this together. But Delta...

And then Commander Theta's words replay in my mind.

Neither of us got what we wanted.

I wanted Ghent safe, and Theta wanted him dead, but *neither of us got what we wanted.*

You won't be the one having his babies now.

I won't be the one, but *someone* will. Some other girl will use his genetic material to breed our species.

The realization sends shock waves through me.

Ghent's alive!

He's in the Bank.

That's why Delta's here.

"Why are you telling me all this?" I ask, afraid I already know the answer.

With a derisive snort at Ma Temple, Delta turns to me. When she speaks, her voice is cold steel. "My son trusts you. We need you to get him away from that hateful place."

Chapter 22

As I glance out Omicron's window, I notice the light beginning to fade. We've been here for almost a full day: Omicron, my mother and I. We talked for a while and then my mother encouraged me to get some sleep for the journey ahead. I've done my best to nap, but I'm too keyed up. My mother is in Omicron's bedchamber watching over her now. I hope I see my grandmother again before we have to leave. It isn't every day you discover a long lost relative, and that she's an Elder to boot.

They told me the story of our family. When she was younger than I am now, only about seven hundred weeks, Omicron discovered she had the rarest of all dual Callings, one that had never been heard of before, or since: Elder and motherhood. She was forced to confide in the Elders of her own time who authorized her to raise a child before she joined their ranks. Omicron says it gave her a unique perspective when she took up her duties as an Elder. She truly understood the fabric of the society, having been a mother herself.

But part of the bargain with her own Elders was that she had to conceal her identity and hide away from her family and friends when she joined their order. When my mother took up with Theta, Omicron believed that her mothering duties were complete. She removed herself from the public eye and took up residence with the Elders. Her contact with my mother was severed. Until Mom ventured outside the wall. Omicron blamed herself for what happened. She felt she should have known what my mother would do, worried that she had injected some of those ideas into Sigma's mind herself: the idea that our society couldn't sustain itself, that there was more outside we needed to find.

Omicron intervened to authorize my birth, and she watched quietly to make sure Mom and I were safe as I grew up. She also had her suspicions about Delta and Epsie. She didn't want to pry in case she made it dangerous for them, but when Epsie was admitted to the Clinic, Omicron had an uneasy feeling. That's when she asked my mother to resume her explorations outside the wall. Omicron needed greater knowledge of the outside so she could offer assistance to Delta and Epsie if it came to that. Unfortunately, it did.

After Ghent turned himself in, Delta had begged Ma Temple to save him. Like her daughter, Ma Temple was affected by Ghent's bravery and Delta's obvious devotion to him. She pretended to go along with Commander Theta's plan to fake Ghent's execution and spirit him away to the Bank for breeding, but she also contacted Omicron who called on my mom to help.

So that's where we are now. Everyone should be in place for tonight's expedition. Ma Temple has spent the day at the Bank preparing to fake Ghent's post-operative infection and subsequent "real" death. Upsilon should be on standby with the vehicle after returning Delta to the Clinic. Delta's cover story is that Upsilon escorted her to her quarters to collect some things for Epsie and then returned her to the Clinic.

Outside the window, a small clutch of bats screeches as they pitch into the sky, wings outstretched. I examine my new clothes. A black outfit, from head to toe, like my mother's. Rubber-soled shoes, lightweight and sturdy. We look like twins.

"Ready, Omega?" Mom's voice startles me as she enters from Omicron's bedchamber. There are dark hollows under her eyes, and I wonder how much rest she's had today.

"Where's Omicron?" I ask, still not quite ready to call her Grandmother.

She motions at the door. "She's getting up now. Don't worry, honey. She'll say goodbye before we leave. Did you get enough sleep? It may be a while before we can rest again." She scrutinizes my face. "Your eyes are bloodshot."

"Yours, too."

She grimaces. "I suppose it's not easy to sleep with all of this going on."

"No, it's not." Omicron's voice crackles from the doorway. We both turn to her. "But you will both do me proud regardless."

The bats outside shriek as the sun disappears beneath the horizon.

"It's time," Mom says, as she moves to the entryway to check our bags. "Throw me your cloak, Omega." I give it to her, and she threads it through the straps of my pack. I tremble at the thought of seeing Ghent again. I can't believe he's alive.

Mom crosses the room to Omicron. "I suppose this is goodbye."

"Never goodbye, my daughter. Only so long." She wraps her arms around Mom and even though Mom stands much taller than she does, she looks like a small child. "Come here, my granddaughter." Omicron beckons me, and I join the embrace. The Elder's arms are surprisingly strong, infusing me with confidence that this might work. Mom breaks away and wipes her palm over her face. I back away too and look at both of them. I can't yet get my mind around the fact that this is my family.

Mom goes to the door and grabs the two packs, handing one to me. "Upsilon should be here any moment."

As if Mom's words conjured her, the door opens and the Protector hurries inside. "All good here?"

"Yes, Private," Omicron says as she limps to the bench where she left her cane earlier. "Thank you for your assistance."

"It's my pleasure. I care about the world my daughters grow up in." Upsilon has a dual Calling? Protector and motherhood?

My mother casts a final glance at Omicron who raises a hand to her heart before she speaks. "My children, you are doing something brave and important. I hope you find sanctuary, and happiness."

Mom gathers my elbow and escorts me through the door, with Upsilon following. As the door closes, I wonder if I hear a sob from Omicron's quarters, but I can't see with the two women behind me. They shepherd me to the entrance where Upsilon's vehicle is parked. The sun has set, and it's difficult to see where we are. The scent of gardenias is strong, but all I can see is a paved pathway and some boulders. The shriek of the bats is more distant now.

After checking that no one is around, Upsilon helps us both into the back seat with our packs before slipping into the driver's seat herself. "The tinted windows will help some, but you both should keep your heads down." Mom nestles down beside me, pressing my head into the seat and covering us both with one of the dark cloaks. The engine hums to life.

Chapter 23

"Are you sure this is the right place?" Mom peers out the back window as Upsilon pulls in behind the only available cover, a small copse of barren trees. It's not a great hiding place, but we won't be here long, at least if all goes to plan. We're somewhere near the eastern boundary of the palisade, away from all the main buildings. The ground is flat with rocks scattered in small piles here and there. There's hardly any grass. It's an area no one comes to visit. There's no reason. Even if they did, there's nothing to see. This place is well hidden in plain sight.

"I scoped it out earlier," Upsilon says from the driver's seat. "There's a steel panel in the ground right here. It leads down to the Bank's back entrance."

I know from our planning session that the Bank is underground. It gives me the creeps to think of all those boys and men stored away down there like produce. As well as the poor women who give birth to them. They take a vow of secrecy and dedicate their lives to male childbearing in solitude. Their families are told they're dead. It's all happening somewhere right here, beneath our feet.

"How far down is it?" I ask.

"I'm not exactly sure, but not too far," my mother says. "The morgue is near the exit. Ma Temple will be waiting for us there."

The morgue. I shudder. "Where do they take them, the men, after they die?"

"Cremation pit. Not far from here." Upsilon points to the south. "Ashes are buried where they won't be found.

I start to hyperventilate.

"Honey?" My mother turns to me, her brow creased. "Here, put your head between your knees." She eases my neck forward.

"I think I'm going to be sick."

Upsilon opens her door and slides out, allowing a burst of

fresh air to bathe the vehicle's interior. That helps a bit. When I get out of the car, Mom is right behind me. She leaves our packs inside the vehicle.

"I know this is scary, Omega. Are you sure you can do this?" Mom sounds really worried. I have to get myself together.

"It's so horrible, Mom. What they're doing here."

"Yes, it is."

A dog barks in the far distance, setting off a round of howling. We don't keep a lot of pets around here. It's too many unnecessary mouths to feed, but the school has some cats and dogs for the younger kids to play with. They've probably left the dogs out in the yard this evening. They do that on most summer nights.

"All clear." I hadn't realized until she spoke that Upsilon had moved away from us to check the area. Metal scrapes against metal as she drops to her knees and begins to shove against the panel flat on the ground. The opening to the Bank. My mother touches my cheek before moving to help her. I follow. The panel is large – about five feet by four. It's heavy, but we manage to move it, exposing a keypad underneath beside a large grate. Upsilon punches in a code and the grate slides open to expose a metal staircase leading down into the facility. Mom and I are going in while Upsilon stands guard.

"Ready?" Upsilon asks.

"As I'll ever be," Mom says. "Omega?"

I nod. Mom slips a tiny flashlight out of her sleeve and snaps it on, illuminating the staircase. "I'll go first. If anything happens to me, come back to Upsilon. She'll get you safely away."

I glance at the two women.

"It'll be fine, Omega." Upsilon claps me on the shoulder. "I'll cover the entrance." She snaps a salute at my mother who grimaces as she lowers her feet to the top step.

She descends into the darkness. The flashlight beam is almost out of sight when she calls out, "All clear, Omega." With a last glance at Upsilon, who is now stationed a few paces back, I allow myself to move forward on shaky feet.

The journey into the Bank seems to take a long time, but that's probably because I keep stumbling on the worn steps. My mother fares better because she's holding the light, but she's also taking the most risk going first. The air is stale. I wonder if the ventilation is any better in the actual quarters where they keep the men. I don't know if I'm relieved or disappointed that I won't get to see it. The morgue sounds horrifying enough without seeing a bunch of men trapped like caged animals underground.

Ma Temple tried to explain earlier that they keep the men as humanely as possible. There are no actual cages, and there's plenty of food and exercise. The bedrooms and shared living facilities are supposedly as well furnished as our own. She assured me that the men grew up never knowing anything different, so to them, this is normal. But they're still prisoners. They can't get out of the Bank. Ever. Not until they die. I think about my own life. Stuck inside the palisade. How different is it really? We're all prisoners in one way or another.

My mother throws her arm back, a signal to stop. "I think we're here." She scrambles forward. Something beeps, followed by the sound of metal grating. "This is it. The morgue. Wait here."

The light disappears. It's pitch black and difficult to breathe. I can't hear a thing. Not my mother's voice. Not the sound of her feet. I take a step to my left and hit a cold stone wall. I brace my palm against it and try to get my breath under control. After what seems like an eternity, the light appears ahead of me, illuminating my mother's features. "I've found it. Come on."

I stumble forward.

"There's no one here," she says.

She grasps my wrist to lead me through a door into a small room. It's hard to get a sense of the full dimensions in the semi-darkness, but the flashlight gives off enough of a glow to see that the walls are made of stone and lined with steel benches. There's a storage locker at the far end, but other than that, the room is empty. And so cold.

My mother snakes an arm around me. "We must have beaten her here. We'll have to wait."

Mom moves to close the door behind us, but I pull her back.

"Omega, I need to close the door. I don't want to raise suspicion if anyone else is around."

Before I can respond, we're interrupted by a squeaking from somewhere down the hall.

"Mom?" I grab her arm and try to pull her out of the doorway.

She grips my shoulders. "It's probably Ma Temple, but just in case, follow me." She leads me to the far wall and pushes me beneath one of the benches. She takes a step away. "I can still see you. Move back." I do as I'm told, feeling the cold of the stone wall seeping into my bones. The squeaking is louder, accompanied by a whirring noise, like wheels on a mobile platform. Mom dives under the shelf beside me, pressing herself back as far as possible. The cold air invades my lungs. The overhead light flickers on in the center of the room. From our hiding place I can make out the wheels and lower struts of a metal gurney.

"Sigma?" A hissed whisper. Ma Temple. I almost crumple with relief.

"Here." My mother straightens out from under the bench motioning for me to stay back. I watch her legs as she approaches the gurney. She takes in a sharp breath and places her feet apart.

"He's going to be alright, Sigma," Ma Temple says. "He had a reaction to the drugs we gave him to fake the post-op infection. I had to give him a sedative."

I can't help it. I dart from my hiding place and push my mother aside. Ma Temple stands at the head of the gurney clad in her white scrubs, but I'm not looking at her. I'm staring at the inert form on the flat metal surface. *Ghent*. He's lying on his back, head lolling to the side and he looks pale and weak. Dark circles surround his eyes. His thick hair has been shorn to a light fuzz.

Sweat beads around his temples. He's wearing loose gray pajamas at least a size too big. His feet are bare and clean. The pajama top is raised to reveal a large bandage around his midsection, padded with gauze.

I step toward Ma Temple, but Mom grabs my elbow and pulls me into her chest.

Ma Temple looks down at Ghent before turning to us. She directs her next words to me. "Omega, please. He'll be fine. I promise. It will take a little longer than we hoped, but we can stick with the original plan. You and your mother will have to continue his medications as well as keeping his incision clean. I'll give you the medical supplies you'll need, but we have to get the boy to the transport first."

My mother's grip loosens. "What's the best way to do this?"

"We can wheel him as far as the back entrance, but you'll have to carry him up the stairs. I'll take the gurney back and put the supplies together for you."

A chill surges through me when I realize that means a second trip down here to get the medicine, but that's the least of our worries right now.

"I'll go first." My mother pushes past Ma Temple and snaps on her flashlight as Ma Temple turns off the overhead light. We move as fast as we can, Ma Temple following my mother's lead. I take up the rear, peering at Ghent's unmoving form. At one point, I reach out to touch his bare toe. It's cold as ice.

It takes a while for us to get to the stairs. This is where the gurney-ride ends.

"Sigma," Ma Temple addresses my mom, "you need to help me get him up." The women gather beside the gurney and my mother extends the flashlight to me. "Here. You hold this."

"No." I wave it away and step in closer.

"We don't have time to argue, Sigma," Ma Temple says grabbing the flashlight. "Let her do it."

With some difficulty, my mother and I maneuver Ghent's limp

form so he's propped up between us with an arm draped over each of our shoulders. Each of us braces his waist. He's dead weight. It's difficult to keep my balance. He doesn't even smell like himself. He gives off a sickly antiseptic odor.

"I've got to get the gurney back," Ma Temple says. "Sigma, can you manage this?" She pushes the light into my mother's free hand. "Come back to the morgue, and I'll have the supplies ready for you."

Mom grunts as we position Ghent at the bottom of the stairs. "Ready, Omega?" She starts to climb. I'm a step behind her most of the way, wobbling under Ghent's weight, but determined not to fail. I can hear the squeak of the gurney disappearing back into the dark tunnel. Ma Temple hasn't turned on any lights. She must be down here often enough to know her way in the dark. It's difficult to maneuver Ghent to the top of the stairs and we have to stop a few times to adjust our grip. I'm relieved when I see the tips of Upsilon's boots at the opening. She leans in to help us get him all the way out.

"He's not looking too good," she says, and I want to scream, but I hold it in. It won't help if I lose control now. We're so close to getting away with this.

"He'll be okay. He needs some meds," my mother says to Upsilon.

We manage to move his inert form out of the stairwell and lay him on the ground beside the metal panel. I reach for his cheek. It's warm, even though his feet are cold.

"Should we get him a blanket?" I ask.

"Let's get him into the vehicle," Mom says.

Upsilon and I take his head and shoulders and Mom lifts his legs. We struggle to get him inside and, when we do, I slide my pack under his head as a pillow.

"I'm going back in for the meds," Mom says.

"I'm coming with." I move to her side.

"No, honey. Stay here with Upsilon. If I'm not back in ten

minutes, get him out of here."

"You think it might be a trap?" Upsilon asks Mom.

"I hope not. I think she's really working with us this time," Mom says, nodding at the opening in the ground.

My heart skips a beat. I'm torn between the need to help Mom and the desire to stay with Ghent.

Mom grins and presses a kiss to my cheek. "It'll be alright, Omega." She seems like a different person now, like an adventurer. Somehow the attitude suits her. She strides to the opening. I follow her and let out a stutter of protest.

She touches my cheek with the pad of her index finger. "I promise everything will be fine, sweetheart, but I need you to stay here for now."

I can feel moisture welling beneath my eyelids but I'm not going to cry. I'm part of this plan and I have to be strong.

"Okay?" she asks.

I nod, not sure if I can control my voice.

"See you soon." She disappears down the stairway.

Chapter 24

"Omega?" Upsilon is calling me from her post beside the vehicle. I hurry back to look at Ghent. Upsilon steps aside so I can lean in through the driver's door and run my fingers over his shaved head. What's left of his hair is prickly. I bite my lip. Shielding my movements from Upsilon, I drop a kiss to his forehead and run my thumb across his cheek, which is now devoid of hair. He murmurs and his fingers twitch. I clasp his hand in mine. "It's going to be alright, Ghent. You're going to be alright." I stand still, staring down at him for what seems like a long time before turning to Upsilon who has slid into the passenger seat and is rummaging around in one of the packs.

"How long has it been?" I ask her.

"About six minutes."

It can't only be six. It feels like forever. We're too exposed. The entry to the Bank is wide open and the vehicle isn't very well hidden. I run the backs of my knuckles over Ghent's cheek. It's still hot. Perspiration beads his forehead. He needs that medicine, and my mom needs me to help her.

"I'm going in after her," I say.

"Sit tight. You heard what she said. She'll only be another minute or so."

But it isn't only another minute. The minute passes. Then another. Then another. The only sound is Ghent's raspy breathing.

I'm leaning through the driver's door, holding his hand and running the pad of my thumb across his bony knuckles when Upsilon speaks. "We need to go. It's time."

"No."

"It's been more than ten minutes."

It's good that Upsilon can't see my face because I don't want her to anticipate what I'm about to do. Pressing a brief kiss to

Ghent's forehead, I dart for the entry to the Bank and am down the steps before she can stop me. She calls out, but doesn't follow. Someone has to stay with Ghent. She knows it, and she'll do it. Otherwise this will all be for nothing.

It's dark in the tunnels. I let my feet guide me to the morgue. I'm almost sure I'm lost when I hear raised voices. More than two of them. I creep forward. That's when I see the light. The morgue door is open, light spilling into the passage ahead of me. The voices are coming from there. My mother and Ma Temple. And someone else I hoped I'd never come across again: Commander Theta.

"Sigma," the commander's tone is icy. "I should have known your questionable loyalties would lead you to something like this. Infiltrating the Bank. What were you planning to achieve?"

"We can't go on like this, Theta. You know we can't. The society is dying," my mother says.

There's the sound of a loud slap, skin on skin. My mother cries out.

"Spare me the rant, Sigma," the commander says. "I've heard it all before, and Med-Tech Temple, I was expecting a body down here. Where is it?"

"Already taken care of, ma'am." Ma Temple's voice sounds formal, as if she expected to confront the commander all along. Did she? Has she sold us out to the Protectorate? I press myself against the wall, hardly daring to breathe. My knees are weak, but I have to hold myself up. If Ma Temple has betrayed us, I need to get out of here and warn Upsilon.

Mom's next words surprise me. "What happened to you, Theta? What have the Protectors done to you?"

"It wasn't the Protectors," the commander snaps back. "It was you. All this is your doing. With all your crazy notions of saving the world, you couldn't even save yourself. Couldn't save what we… The two of you had better come with me."

The commander's words are followed by a scuffle.

I slap my hand over my mouth to stop myself screaming. I cower into the shadows as two figures emerge from the morgue, my mother and Ma Temple. Both of them have their hands clasped in front of them. My mother's wrists are bound with a length of cord, but I can't see Ma Temple's. My mother is blocking her from my view. She's scanning the tunnel. Looking for me? I want to cry out, but I don't dare move. I have to get back to Upsilon.

Mom stumbles forward. Then I see why. Commander Theta has shoved her in the shoulder and is forcing her down the tunnel, away from me. The commander is clutching my mother's flashlight, illuminating their path from behind. Ma Temple walks slightly beside and behind my mother. She doesn't speak or look at either of the other women. I can't tell if she's working with Theta or not, but if she is, why did she lie about Ghent?

As they disappear into the blackness, my mother shoots a glance over her shoulder. I have no idea if she can see me or not, and I can't risk any movement. Is it my imagination or does her gaze dart toward the back exit? Is she telling me to go? She knows I can't leave her here. I won't. Maybe she's telling me to get Upsilon. Or maybe it's only my imagination. Theta presses the flashlight into her back and forces her forward. Until I can't see them anymore.

I steady myself against the wall and try to calm down. There's no choice but to go back the way I came. Alert Upsilon and come up with a plan to save Mom. It's dark again. They turned off the light when they left the morgue, but I know the way now. With my hand braced against the wall to guide me, I turn and start walking. I only manage a few steps before someone grabs me from behind and a hand clamps over my mouth. I kick out, almost managing to dislodge my attacker, but the grip tightens. Then I notice the scent.

Honeysuckle.

"Calm down, Omega. It's only me. I'm going to let go now.

Don't scream, okay?"

Suddenly free, I whirl around as a small flashlight snaps on, illuminating Gamma's familiar features.

"Surprise," she says.

I'm too stunned to react as she grabs me by the arm and drags me toward the morgue. I start to resist, but she's insistent. "They're gone, Omega. We're okay." The morgue is empty now. Gamma rushes to the locker at the far end of the room and starts rummaging around inside.

"What are you doing?"

When she closes it, she's wielding a burlap sack. "The medical supplies we need. For the *deman*."

"What's going on?"

"I'm the back-up plan," Gamma says proudly, indicating the sack slung over her shoulder. "My mother told me everything. I know she didn't kill the *deman*, that you're breaking him out of here. I offered to help. She wanted to keep me out of it, but I think she finally realized she might need a Plan B. So here I am." She indicates the door with the flashlight. "We should move. We don't have much time."

"Wait a second." I take a few steps away from her, further into the morgue. "My mother's in danger. I can't leave her."

"It's going to be alright." Gamma's poised at the door. "My mother sent a message to Omicron. Your mom will be alright."

Gamma knows about Omicron?

"Even if that's true, why would you want to help us?" I wrap my arms around myself.

She settles the sack on the floor and approaches me. "Because I want to actually meet a real live *deman*. In the flesh. This is a once-in-a-lifetime opportunity, you know." She's closer now. I take a step back and bump into the edge of one of the benches.

"This isn't a joke, Gamma. If we do this, there's no turning back," I say. "You might never see your mother again. You might never see anyone again. We might all end up dead."

"I know, and I'm with you." She lifts my hand and squeezes it, reminding me of the way I touched Ghent not so long ago in the vehicle outside. Part of me wishes I could go back in time, back to when Gamma and I were school friends drinking hot chocolate, playing schoolyard pranks, and we didn't know the truth about anything.

Without any warning, Gamma rises to her toes and presses her lips to mine, hard and fast. The scent of honeysuckle overwhelms me before she takes a step back and looks deep into my eyes. "Whatever happens, I'm on your side, Omega."

"Why?" I grasp the edges of the bench so tight that my fingernails make a scraping sound along the metal.

"Do I really need to answer that?" She grins in that familiar way of hers.

This could be the worst idea ever.

"Anyway," she continues, "what choice do you have? The *deman's* in a bad way and you'll never manage the wastelands without help."

Chapter 25

In the end, Gamma's right. I have no choice. Upsilon can't come outside the walls, and I need someone to help with Ghent. It was going to be my mother, but that won't happen now. My heart sinks at the thought of what the commander will put my mother through before Omicron can get to her. But Upsilon is already on her way. As soon as Gamma and I got to the transport with the supplies, we told her everything and she took off after Mom. Gamma and I had to move forward, to get Ghent away before anyone reports us missing.

We can only take the vehicle as far as the wall. There's no way to get it outside and, even if we could, it would be too easy to trace, and we'd have no way to recharge it. Gamma has ditched her communicator too. Upsilon is going to report the vehicle stolen and hope they believe her story about some girls stealing it and taking it on a joy ride. We'll have to make our way outside on foot. Hopefully, Ghent will be strong enough to walk soon. For now we'll need to help him, and carry the packs. The vehicle is stopping and starting on the overgrown path. Gamma has never driven before. I'm in the back with Ghent, trying to rearrange the packs so they're as light as possible. We're dumping anything that isn't essential so we can manage Ghent and the medicine.

We hit another deep rut. Ghent slides on the seat and groans. I drop the packs to my feet so I can check on him. I feel his forehead. It might be my imagination, but it seems a little cooler. With any luck the fever is breaking. Gamma's mother gave her instructions about how to administer the medications, and we managed to get one of the painkillers into him before we took off.

The car lurches to a stop, and I'm thrown into the seat in front, my body blocking Ghent's from harm. I settle him back, and grit my teeth. "Gamma, what're you doing?"

I can only see the back of her head, but she sounds amazed. "We found it."

The driver's door opens and the flashlight sparks. I lean forward to see Gamma standing outside and training the beam on the bramble-covered gate in the wall. Gamma sticks her head into the car, pupils dilated. "We're going to make it, Omega."

She examines Ghent's inert form. "Hmm, *demen.* Who would've thought? Not so scary after all." She's been this way since she first saw Ghent. Making a show of how unimpressed she is, but I think she's kind of awed. I remember how scared I felt when I first saw him, although that person was nothing like the pitiful form with his head propped in my lap. His stubbly hair pokes through my trousers and scratches my skin.

Gamma reaches into the vehicle. "Pass me the packs. I'll get them to the gate and try to open it. You get the boy out of the car." Ghent groans and nuzzles his cheek into my thigh. "I think he likes you," she says.

I'm guessing she hasn't figured out exactly how much he likes me. Or how much I like him back. I wonder how she'll react when she finds out. If he lives long enough for that to happen.

I lift the packs to Gamma, making sure the snaps are fastened. They're sturdy canvas, courtesy of Omicron. They should last us for a while, even in poor terrain. My mother already gave me directions to a shallow riverbed she located on her last trip. As long as the water's flowing, she said, it's safe to drink. And there's a trail of brush to give us cover most of the way. We should be able to make it there in a day, and we have enough water in our packs to last until then. Gamma grabs the bags and heads for the wall with the flashlight. I silently watch her start picking away the brambles to clear the gate. They look like they're growing there naturally but I know my mother arranged them that way when she came back inside yesterday. Gamma calls out over her shoulder, "Any time you want to get your butt over here and help, Omega, would be great."

"Coming!" I call, as I pull myself out of the car and brace my arms under Ghent's shoulders to hoist him out. He's heavier than I realized. I haven't had to lift him on my own, and I strain under his weight, only managing to get him seated on the ground, propped against the vehicle. I take a step back. It physically hurts to see him like this. I'm going to need Gamma's help to lift him. I turn to call for her, when I hear his voice.

"Meg?" It's thin and reedy, but it's him. I whirl around, and he's lifting a hand to me even though his eyes are closed. The motion is jerky and his forehead creases with the effort, but he knows I'm here. I drop to my knees and his arm collapses in my lap.

Oh Ghent. It takes all my self-control not to throw my arms around him. He looks so fragile, but he knows I'm here. "Ghent?" I keep my voice as steady as possible, not wanting to frighten him. "Ghent, I'm here. It's going to be alright."

"Meg." His voice is a little stronger. His eyes blink open, searching in the darkness for my face. When he finds it, he stares deep into my eyes. And it really is him. Despite the pale skin and the sweat pooling around his collar. He's alive, and he's going to be okay. If it's the last thing I do, I'm going to make sure of that.

"Did anyone ever tell you, you have beautiful eyes?" He sighs, and his lips quirk into a semblance of his old smile, right side curving higher than the left. "My Meg."

Then he sinks back against the car, his eyes drifting shut.

I'm going to get him out of this. I'm going to keep us safe. Somehow. We're all still alive and we're going to make it. We're going to get out of here. If there's a sanctuary out there, we'll find it. Gathering all my strength, I loop his arm over my shoulders and haul him to his feet. His head lolls into my neck, but he's holding some of his own weight now. His facial fur prickles my skin, reminding me of what he said to me at the reflection pool. He's a different gender, not a different species. Even Gamma knows he's a real person just like us.

If we can all understand that our similarities are more important than our differences, maybe we'll make it, find somewhere safe and free to live. And maybe we'll convince others that we should all pull together somehow.

Perhaps we'll even come back someday and share what we've found … outside the palisade.

Acknowledgments

This is the part where I get to thank everyone who helped me create this story and, as I knew would be the case, I don't know where to start and I know I'm going to leave out tons of folks who were highly instrumental in this book getting written and published. Family must be thanked first because my tribe puts up with a mom who works and writes full time. So to Patrick, Sean, Brianne, and Megan go my thanks for their support and understanding

In terms of the writing itself, I'd be nowhere without my writing instructors and critique groups. This story started out in the first novel writing class I ever took, a young adult writing course taught by Molly Breen. Molly is quite simply the best, and it's impossible to put into words how wonderful it's been to enjoy her teaching, support, and advice over the years on this and other projects. While Molly is a hard act to follow, Annemarie O'Brien picked up the slack in her young adult writing course and gave me endless support which continues to this day.

Thanks also to the instructors in the Fiction Writing Certificate program at UCLA who helped me along the way, especially Jessica Barksdale Inclán who knocked this manuscript (and my psyche) into shape at the last minute when I was ready to throw up my hands in despair. Thanks also to the rest of the UCLA crew I worked with on this project: Robert Eversz, Caroline Leavitt, and a big shout-out to amazing speculative fiction author Alyx Dellamonica who worked through an early draft of the manuscript and taught me to get the adult characters out of the way. If anyone thinks there are still too many adults clogging up the plot, it's definitely on me.

The gals in the Katy Critique Group in Houston were invaluable in keeping my spirits up and keeping me going even when they didn't understand why anyone would write about an all-female society where the lead character had weird eyes for no apparent reason. So thanks, hugs and kisses to Maria Ashworth, Dee Leone, Elena Radulescu, Tina Wissner, Kathy Slaughter, Monica Shaughnessy, and Mandy Broughton. Some of my beta readers who I thank from the bottom of my heart for reading through (often multiple) drafts were Cassandra Robertson, Deborah Halverson, Wendy Nelson-Tokunaga, and Ann Gronvold.

While I know I've left many people out, most of them are either friends from Stanford, UCLA, or SCBWI, so I'm hoping that this big general thank you to those institutions will suffice. Feel free to email and yell at me if I should've mentioned you by name and I didn't.

And of course thanks to the folks at John Hunt/Lodestone for taking a chance on yet another new author, especially to Maria Moloney for her copy-editing expertise.

To my readers, thanks for giving me a chance. If you enjoyed the book and want to find out more about what I'm up to, please visit my website (kcmaguire.com) where you can follow me on Facebook or Twitter, or drop me a line via email. If you enjoyed the book, please consider leaving a review on Goodreads or Amazon, and if you didn't, please let me know. I'll always be a student of writing and will be grateful for any feedback.

K C Maguire
February 2, 2015

Lodestone Books is a new imprint, which offers a broad spectrum of subjects in YA/NA literature. Compelling reading, the Teen/Young/New Adult reader is sure to find something edgy, enticing and innovative. From dystopian societies, through a whole range of fantasy, horror, science fiction and paranormal fiction, all the way to the other end of the sphere, historical drama, steam-punk adventure, and everything in between. You'll find stories of crime, coming of age and contemporary romance. Whatever your preference you will discover it here.